A Supersleuth is Born

A Supersleuth is Born

3-D Vision Mystery Series, Book 1

3-D Vision Mystery Series

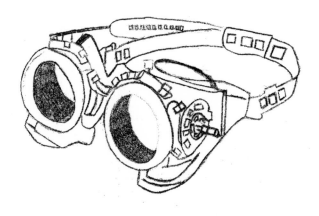

T. Mara Jerabek

A SUPERSLEUTH IS BORN
3-D VISION MYSTERY SERIES, BOOK 1

This is a work of fiction. All of the characters, names, incidents, organizations, and dialogue in this novel are either the products of the author's imagination or are used fictitiously.

iUniverse books may be ordered through booksellers or by contacting:

iUniverse
1663 Liberty Drive
Bloomington, IN 47403
www.iuniverse.com
1-800-Authors (1-800-288-4677)

Because of the dynamic nature of the Internet, any web addresses or links contained in this book may have changed since publication and may no longer be valid. The views expressed in this work are solely those of the author and do not necessarily reflect the views of the publisher, and the publisher hereby disclaims any responsibility for them.

Any people depicted in stock imagery provided by Thinkstock are models, and such images are being used for illustrative purposes only. Certain stock imagery © Thinkstock.

ISBN: 978-1-4917-7488-5 (sc)
ISBN: 978-1-4917-7490-8 (hc)
ISBN: 978-1-4917-7489-2 (e)

Library of Congress Control Number: 2015913400

Print information available on the last page.

iUniverse rev. date: 09/24/2015

CONTENTS

To my son Jessie Nicholas,
who triggered the idea for this book
with his inquisitive mind full of questions and a never-ending
need for answers

Sometimes as I walk
Along this path of my life,
I shall concentrate on the good things
And little on what may not be right.

For although I've had some rough times,
I will look beyond the pain,
And I will look for the rainbow
After the storm and the rain.

For now, even just a glimmer of sun
Can change my point of view
In order to "see" what needs to be done
And all that I must go through.

The path my life has taken
Is viewed from where I stand,
But I shall now look at life from all directions
With my newfound friend.

I find myself in this mystery,
My feet standing in a new place,
And I shall look to solving
This mystery I now face.

For if my life had no detours,
No side streets on its map,
I may not have been given this mystery to solve
If I had not traveled down this unchosen path.

So as I keep my eyes wide open
With a new vision for me to see,
I shall travel each new mile,
And I shall do it skillfully.

—Ethan, supersleuth

PROLOGUE

My relationship with the police started when I was just a kid. Well, actually, I'm still just a kid—eleven, twelve in a couple of months, and in the sixth grade at Green Acres Elementary. To be super honest, it all started with our school resource officer and that Mikey McGurren. Yeah, Mikey. And then, out of nowhere, the situation led to the police. It's almost unbelievable when you hear all about it.

But stop right there! Don't go jumping to any conclusions. It's not what you think. I guess if I were you, I could come up with about a zillion things that kids like me could have done to get a face-to-face with the police, but trust me—it's all good. No, not good—Great, with a capital G.

There are just two really important details that you need to know about me from the start that make my story even more interesting: I'm blind, and I've always wanted to be a supersleuth— you know, a superhero, a crime-solver extraordinaire. Batman, Superman, and Spider-Man all rolled up into one rare creature: me!

You know how life sometimes just moves along at a snail's pace, as slow as they say turtles move, and nothing great ever seems to happen? Well, that's been my life in a nutshell. It's the same old routine, day in and day out: school, homework, some free time, and bed. Are your days like that too? It becomes one big yawn, only to start over again each day—same thing, different day. Well, I wanted more!

When this week started out, I had no idea what was about to happen, and boy, was I in for the shock of my life. Out of nowhere, *wham-bam*, my life changed for good. It's nothing I could have prepared for, nothing I could have imagined happening, and when you hear all about it, I just know you're going to nod in agreement, and you may even be a bit jealous. I'll understand if you are.

It's a tale all right, but this is no "once upon a time" kind of story. You could say it's epic—yeah, that's it, epic, right up there with Great! So here goes my story.

CHAPTER 1

THE TROUBLES IN SCHOOL

"Get up, Ethan! You'll be late again," Allymom called upstairs. I could hear her in the kitchen, and I knew it was morning by the smells of breakfast reaching me. Moms are like that, always worried about you and at the same time making you do things you just really don't want to do. I knew I had to get up, but I really didn't want to.

"I'm up, I'm up!" I yelled down to her. I could still hear her moving around in the kitchen below me.

I let out a great big yawn. It was Tuesday, and the same routine was going to replay. It was like what Allymom had told me about records back in her day: when the needle of the record player got stuck, it played the same part of the song over and over, until you nudged it forward. I felt like that, like my life needed a little nudge to get it moving again. I wanted to be something more than I was. I didn't want to be like yesterday; I wanted to be bright and shiny like the new day. I just didn't know how to do it—yet.

"Ethan, you sure you're up?" Allymom yelled again as I came downstairs and walked into the kitchen.

"Yes, my dearest Allymom." I smiled a big toothy grin as I reached for my breakfast sandwich on the kitchen table. Routine was the name of my game, and I think that's what I disliked most.

"Oh, before I forget, you won't need to wait for Addison today. Her mom called me last night to let me know she'd be staying home sick today, has a cold and a bit of a fever. So go right to Mrs. Pickens's house after school today, Ethan. No exploring and getting into trouble." There was that "mom worry" again.

"I know, I know," I said with a big smile on my face. For some reason, I always needed to say things twice to Allymom, maybe because I hoped it would assure her that I would do whatever she asked me to, and on most days, I did.

"Bye, Allymom," I said. The back door slammed behind me as I left the house and set off for school.

With Addison staying home today, I was on my own and would walk to school alone. This didn't happen often, but it was something I could easily do, although having Addison at my side was always a good thing. I had tools to get me to school safely, as safely as someone with sight. Besides, living in Tonawanda, New York, was about as safe as you could get in today's world.

I punched the button on my audible watch. "Seven forty-five," the electronic voice said. I was right on time.

My school, Green Acres, has been around forever, and it smells like it too—musty and stale. It smells, you know, old. Allymom went to this school too, and so did so many of my friends' parents, so you get the picture: it's old. It's a mammoth reddish brick building with lockers that scream for oil every time you open them to get your books and stuff out. Like I said, this school has been around forever.

I reached the school grounds in no time and went through the back doors. "Morning, Ethan," Sergeant Bailey called out, offering his usual morning greeting.

"Hey there, Sarge," I said back. The school resource officer and I were best buds, I guess you could say, but it was a complicated friendship, since I seemed to get in trouble a little bit more than you'd expect me to, but then, it was not always my fault either.

This day was no different, and before I knew it, *wham-bam*, I found myself sitting outside the principal's office in front of Mrs. Singlebutt's desk, after just taking a few steps through the front door and into the hallway that leads to my homeroom.

When I think back on it, I couldn't have been inside even a minute or two. This was definitely not where I had planned to be when I woke up this morning, and it was not what Allymom would want to hear about when I got home from school. But then again, it was not exactly out of the ordinary for me either. For some reason, I had many personal appearances with the principal, a front-row seat in his office—kind of strange when you think about it, with my being blind and all.

But I'm getting off track. I was nervous, I guess, wondering whether I was in trouble again. It's never a good thing when you're invited to the principal's office. I had a feeling that this was a party I'd rather not have been invited to. There would be no games and definitely no presents at this party.

"Ethan, would you please stop kicking my desk?" Mrs. Singlebutt, the principal's secretary, said. Her southern accent dripped out of her mouth like warm honey, but I never let that sweet voice fool me. It usually meant business, and she was not to be messed with. I didn't know what she looked like, but she sounded short and chubby to me, and her perfume was always in a constant fight with the herbal tea she drank. There was no winner in that fight, and I had a nose to prove it.

"Oops, sorry. I didn't even realize I was doing it, Mrs. Singlebutt. Nerves, I guess." Moving myself back in the chair, I tried to sit as straight as the soldiers Sergeant Bailey always talked about. The cold, hard back of the office chair sent goose bumps down my spine and arms. *Brrr.* I could hear the ticks of a clock over my head, beating off the seconds till my meeting with the principal. My fingers tapped along with the beat.

"There's no need for sorry, Ethan. Just stop doing it," Mrs. Singlebutt said slowly, the sound of her typing on the computer syncing with each word she spoke, letting me know she was busy. The strong smell of her jasmine tea tickled my nose, and I let out a big sneeze.

"Bless you, Ethan," she said, not missing a beat with her typing. I could feel my heart beating fast, following the rhythm of the keys she was hitting.

"I hope your blessing is all I'll need, Mrs. Singlebutt." My voice sounded strange to me, all jittery and stuttering.

"Hmm," Mrs. Singlebutt responded. Somehow that didn't give me the reassurance I was looking for.

Others would assume I wouldn't find myself in the principal's office as much as I do. I have often wondered why. This was the third time for the week, and it was only Tuesday. Gosh darn that Mikey McGurren. If he wasn't bullying me, he was getting me a front-row seat in the principal's office, where I had to defend my innocence with the school resource officer breathing down my neck. His breath was almost as bad as the way Mikey smelled.

My disability has given me a supersleuth of a nose. Sometimes I've thought that if I weren't a kid, I could have been a police dog, the kind that can sniff out anything. A well-trained German shepherd—that's what I'd be, with a bark worse than my bite. This went along with my dream of wanting to be a superhero one day. Supersleuths were cool, and I wanted to be cool.

The loud boom of the principal's office door hitting the back wall made me jump in my seat and brought me back to reality. The roar of his voice made me sit up even straighter in my chair. The earth seemed to shake whenever he talked; I pictured his voice making a larger crevice in the geological fault line, the state of California teetering toward the Pacific Ocean with each word he spoke. My heart raced, and my pulse echoed in my ears. *Boom, boom, boom.* I immediately placed both hands underneath my legs to stop the nervousness that was building in them.

"Ethan, you may come in now," Principal Robertson said in his Darth Vader voice. Whenever Principal Robertson spoke, I had the immediate urge to stick my fingers in both ears to muffle the sound a bit, but I knew that would only make things worse for me.

I felt a large hand on my shoulder before the principal spoke again. It felt like a giant claw, like what a bear's claw would feel like. I didn't know exactly what a bear really looked like, but I had a feeling I was right. I was his captured prey, and his office was the animal trap. Swallowing hard, I squirmed in my chair, trying to push back the fear that was creeping upward from his grasp. *Did I just hear him growl?*

"Ethan, the SRO is here too; you know Sergeant Bailey. Both of us would like to hear the details of this latest interaction between Michael and yourself." Sergeant Bailey was a police officer from the Tonawanda Police Department and our school resource office. Allymom said that in her day, they never needed police officers in the school. I never knew quite how to respond to her whenever she brought that up.

"After we have had our little chat, we will then talk to Michael for his side of the story." I heard what sounded like a chair being pulled out, and I had a picture in my head of the gentle giant sitting down in his giant bear chair. I swear I heard the chair groan. As I swallowed hard, I thought, *Bears don't chat, do they?*

"Okay, sir," I said, my voice quivering. My hands were damp with sweat, and I quickly wiped them on the side of my pants. Even without sight, I could feel all eyes on me, burning little holes into my shirt. *Pow, pow, pow!* I kept repeating silently to myself,

You're innocent, you're innocent, you're innocent, as the sound of a gavel echoed in my ears, warning me of my possible fate.

"Well, sir, you see, uh ... it was like this. I was walking to my first class, and usually, I have Addison with me. She walks with me every day." That's another one of those "mom" things. "You know, she's the girl that helps me throughout the day. Well, today, she's not here. She woke up with a cold or something."

"Yes, Ethan, go on." The voice of Sergeant Bailey sent a chill up my spine again. It reminded me of that old Clint Eastwood movie I had on audiotape. Just by his tone, I could hear those words in my head: *Make my day.*

"Anyway ... I was walking along. I use the lockers on the wall to sometimes guide me, and I know how many steps it takes me to get to each class, forty-four to be exact to get to my first class. I count steps, and I use my voice-activated stepometer, but you know that, right?" I didn't hesitate and kept on talking. Allymom always tells me that when I am nervous, I ramble on and on.

"Well, my uncle Nick, Allymom's brother, invented it for me. He works in technology in Silicon Valley, out there in California. It's still in the planning stages, but so far it works super-duper, and he has high hopes for it. He creates all this really neat stuff. Well, this stepometer is like a pedometer. It's programmed with all the places I frequently go and has a GPS device inside it, kind of a MapQuest for the blind."

I heard Principal Robertson clear his throat and realized I'd gone off-topic again.

"Well, then all of a sudden, I swear out of nowhere, I tripped over something, and the next thing I knew, I was falling. I hit something—well, someone—and felt us both falling. I knew it was Mikey right away," I said.

"Now, Ethan, what made you realize it was Michael?" Principal Robertson asked.

"Well, sir, I don't know if you ever noticed it or not, but he smells like an onion."

I heard a soft chuckling sound, which abruptly ended. Principal Robertson cleared his throat and then spoke. "Hmm, I never noticed that, Ethan. Then what?"

"Well, I felt him shove me off him, and I fell into the lockers. Then I heard Sergeant Bailey's voice calling out both our names. I don't think Mikey meant any harm this time, sir."

"Okay, Ethan, if you don't have anything further to add, Sergeant Bailey will show you to your seat outside my office. We will talk to Michael now."

As the door opened, the whiff of onion reached my nose, and I knew Mikey was close.

"Hey, P-Pero, you'd b-better not have th-thrown me under the b-bus," Mikey stuttered as he went by me. Mikey always called me by my last name; I think he did it just to aggravate me. But it rolled off me just like that smell rolled off him.

"That'll be enough, Michael," the SRO said firmly. Nothing slipped by Sergeant Bailey. His ears were as good as, if not better than, mine. He told me this was because he had been a sniper shooter in the Vietnam War, and there you had to be vigilant not just with your eyes but also with your ears. He told me he had telescopic vision, and I remember thinking, *I want that too.*

The sounds of the door closing and the muffled voices made my hands start to sweat again, and I let out a slow, steady breath, trying to calm my nerves. I could only imagine the tale Mikey was conjuring up to get me in trouble. That was the game played here; he was always either trying to get out of trouble or trying to get me into it. Mikey's dad was the mayor in our town, and I was sure he didn't want his dad coming down to school again. I guessed it must be hard to be Mikey at times.

I could hear Mrs. Singlebutt still at her desk, typing on her computer. Out of habit, and still feeling nervous, I accidentally kicked her desk with my swinging foot. The typing came to an abrupt halt.

"Eeeethan." She said my name slowly, stretching it out like a rubber band, and before I could even get out an "I'm sorry," she began typing again, silencing me before I could speak.

It seemed like forever before the door opened again, the gentle creaking pulling me out of my own thoughts.

"Boys, you can both return to your classes. Michael seems to tell the same story as you do, Ethan. I don't want to see you boys again anytime soon. Let's not make a habit of this. Do I make myself clear?"

"Yes, sir," we both responded at the same time. I was kind of shocked that Mikey hadn't made up some story to get me into trouble. That should have been my first clue that this day was going to be different. I knew Mikey was standing close by my side. My nose gave me confirmation, and then I felt the hard nudge of his elbow into my rib, which seemed to go unnoticed by the principal, and I stayed silent with the pain. Superheroes do not cry.

"Sergeant Bailey will make sure you get to your next class, Ethan. If your teachers need further explanation, please have them call me. Let's have a good week, boys."

Sergeant Bailey placed his hand on my shoulder again, leading me out of the office. I tripped again, and my shoulder hit what felt like the wall.

"You okay, Son?" Sergeant Bailey asked.

I knew by how close that onion smell was to me that Mikey somehow had got the chance to trip me up once again.

"Have a nice t-trip. See you next f-fall," Mikey said so quietly in my ear that even the sergeant didn't hear this time.

"I'm fine, sir," I said, despite knowing what had just happened. By some miracle, it had gone unnoticed by Sergeant Bailey again. Twice in one day. Mikey and I used to be friends when we were younger, but now he was my archnemesis, and he would be until I could think of something that could turn things around for me and become the superhero I had always dreamed I could be. Little did I know it was lurking right around the next corner of my life.

CHAPTER 2

WALK TO PICKENS'S

The rest of the school day zoomed by with no problems, and the clanging of the last bell signaled the end of the day. Thankfully, I had stayed out of the principal's office.

Whenever I made my way out the back door, Sergeant Bailey was always close by, making sure I got out safely. *Yippee!* I thought as I passed through the door. *Hello to freedom and fresh air. Adios to musty and rusty.*

"You be careful out there, my little soldier," Sergeant Bailey said. It was like a mantra to him.

"Aye aye, sir." I smiled as the words left my mouth. I felt like one of the soldiers he always talked about from his time spent in the marines and in Vietnam. My hand went up in salute, just as he had taught me.

"At ease, soldier," Sergeant Bailey responded, and I could hear the smile in his voice.

With my backpack, stepometer, and walking stick and homework that would take an hour or two to get done, I made the trek home—well, to Mrs. Pickens's house. I hated carrying the stick, almost as much as I hated doing homework. Allymom made me carry it, and I did it just for her, but I never used it. I felt like it said to the world, "There's something different about this

10

kid," and I didn't want to be just different. I wanted to be super different. Super different and cool—yeah, that's exactly what I wanted.

Sounds of the school kids yelling and laughing rang in my ears as I walked past the school playground. Balls were bouncing, and sneakers made rubbery sounds as they hit the pavement while the rest of the kids played after-school games before making their way home too. These were the familiar sounds I heard every day, so my ears recognized them, just as a seeing person's eyes would recognize daily sights.

"Later, Ethan!" Greg Tatter yelled out.

"See ya, Ethan." The sweet, shy voice of Shira Zillerbee was barely above a whisper.

"Later, gator."

"Adios, Ethan."

"Bye, Ethan!"

"See ya, dude."

As more kids yelled my name, I stopped to wave my good-byes to them, another salute until the next day.

"Steps resumed," my stepometer alerted me. I continued on my way, the clicks of my stepometer resuming like the metronome of my life, keeping beat with my steps. *Tick, tick, tick.*

I was on my way to Mrs. Pickens's house, my usual after-school routine. When Allymom was working at the *Tonawanda Tribune*, where she was a top-notch reporter, I went to Mrs. Pickens's house, a few doors down from where we lived. "Better safe than sorry. I wasn't a latchkey kid, and neither will you be." Allymom's words rang in my head. It made me smile to myself to recall them, but I always thought, *A latch-what?*

The way home was always the same. Thirty-three steps out the school's exit door, a left turn, 275 steps straight ahead, another left, and fifty-five steps to Mrs. Pickens's back door. I wondered how many steps someone actually took in a lifetime. Have you ever wondered that too?

"Howdy, Ethan." I recognized Mr. Smergle's voice right away as I made my way home. His cat, Lucy, let out a soft purr of a hello as I passed. He was one of Allymom's assigned lookouts. He came out on his porch every time I passed by on my way home from school.

"Hey, Mr. Smergle," I said as I continued on my way. We generally just exchanged a quick hello; we never had a long conversation.

"Hello, Ethan," Mrs. Frangle said as I kept walking, and I waved in the direction of her voice. The flowers from her garden filled the air like a big flower-power cloud. The smell was so strong that at times I felt like I was suffocating. It was almost as bad as when Allymom put on too much perfume. Yuck!

"*Buon pomeriggio*, Ethan," said Mrs. Catalano, the scents of basil and spaghetti sauce oozing from her house. She was always cooking something, and it always smelled great. Those smells always made me feel hungry, even if I had just eaten.

"Ciao, Mrs. Catalano," I responded back with a wave in her direction, my stomach growling in unison.

"Hey, P-Pero. Whatcha d-doing?" Mikey lived next door to Mrs. Catalano and always seemed to be around when I left school too. I don't think Allymom asked him to look out for me, but that's just a hunch.

"See ya t-tomorrow in s-school. Hope you liked the t-trip I sent you on today. Did you take p-pictures?" Mikey's laugh reminded me of the Joker from *Batman*. He always made it sound evil and menacing. I don't know which was worse: the way he laughed or the way he smelled. I think it would be a tie if it came down to a vote. Staring, unblinking, in the direction of his voice, I stayed silent and kept walking.

The sounds of a bike whizzing by and the ring of a bike bell let me know Tony S. was close by. The smells of rust and bike grease filled the air around me. Yes, rust does smell a certain way, kind of like dying metal. Weird, I know, but strange as it sounds, those smells were associated with Tony S., and so it was all good, in a smelly sort of way. Tony S. was a homeless man who lived in the town of Tonawanda. Everyone knew him. Allymom told me our town had offered him assistance, even a place to stay, but Tony S. liked living on the streets. He said it made him feel freer, probably the same type of feeling I had when leaving school.

"Yo, Ethan," Tony S. yelled to me as he went by. He always seemed to be around when I made my way home from school too. I think he checked on me too, just because that's who he was. Sergeant Bailey told me Tony was a Vietnam vet too. He called him "a casualty of the war" and said that they actually had grown up together and had gone to the same school. It's funny how two people can turn out so different.

"Yo, back to you, Tony," I yelled back to him, the distant sound of his bicycle alerting me to the fact that he was already well past me. The faint sound of his bike bell signaled his good-bye.

"Hi there, young man."

Recognizing the voice of Mr. Goodsmith, I knew I was just about halfway to Mrs. Pickens's house. Mr. Goodsmith was like a grandfather to me. He had impressed me from the first time I met him, and I was always ready and willing to believe anything and everything he ever told me. Allymom said he was well into his seventies. Eek! That's old. A metalworker in his younger days, he had made a lot of the town's statues, but now he just filled his time making wind chimes from old scrap-metal parts, which he then sold from his front porch. He once had described each of them to me in detail, including the different sounds they made. I thought that was so cool.

"How was school today, Ethan?" he asked.

"Same old, same old," I said, hoping I sounded convincing.

"Hmm ... you sure about that?" There was a hint of doubt in his voice. How did adults always know when kids weren't being totally up front with them? It was like they had this sixth sense or internal radar: *Alert, alert. Fib ahead.*

"Mr. Goodsmith, I swear you have some hidden camera at my school you're not telling me about." We both laughed. "Well, you know that Mikey McGurren, the mayor's son?"

"Is that young man still giving you trouble?" he said worriedly.

"Well ... kinda. We had a bit of an, you could say, altercation at the start of school."

"Altercation—now that's a ten-dollar word if I ever heard one," Mr. Goodsmith said.

"Yeah, *altercation* is the word Sergeant Bailey used." I went on to tell him all that had happened, and he stayed silent for a minute after I finished.

"Ethan, it is easier to live one's life with honesty than with deception. It is easier to be a friend than an enemy. Maybe you just need to figure out how to make Mikey your friend again. You remember he once was a few years back, and you two couldn't be separated. Show him that all this bullying nonsense has no effect on you, and hopefully, he will either leave you alone or become a friend to you once again."

I thought about this for a while, thinking back to the days Mikey and I had been inseparable, and I couldn't seem to pinpoint where it all had gone wrong. Mr. Goodsmith might be right about Mikey, but I wasn't buying it for now. Maybe it all came down to us growing up and going our separate ways, living different lives, like Sergeant Bailey and Tony S.

"Well, thanks, Mr. Goodsmith. I better be on my way. Homework is waiting," I said with a groan.

After a few more steps, I opened the back screen door to Mrs. Pickens's house and heard her singing a song. Her singing always alerted me to just where she was, although I never recognized any songs she sang.

"Hey there, Mrs. Pickens," I said.

"What's cookin', good lookin'?" In addition to singing and humming, Mrs. Pickens was fond of quirky sayings, and she sang those too.

"Grillin' and chillin'. Grillin' and chillin', Mrs. P."

We both laughed.

Mrs. Pickens had been the local librarian at one time, for over forty years. Now she just worked every now and then.

"Well, Ethan, do you mind if I run down to the store for just a minute? I saw this great recipe today on the food channel, and I just can't wait to make it," she said eagerly.

If Mrs. Pickens wasn't making a new recipe, she was rearranging the furniture after watching an episode on the home and garden channel. Since I was blind, the rearranging of furniture wasn't a good thing for me, and I had the bumps and bruises to prove it.

"Nah, go ahead, Mrs. Pickens. I'm going into the den to start on my homework."

I heard the back screen door slam shut as I made my way out of the kitchen and into the den, my haven in her house. I felt my foot catch on something that hadn't been there yesterday, and my outstretched arms flapped like a bird's wings as I tried to regain my balance. This was going to hurt—I just knew it—and there was no stopping me. The fall was inevitable. The side of my face hit something cold and hard, buffered somewhat by my flailing arms, and I screamed out loud to the TV gurus, "Darn you, home and garden channels!" And that's the last thing I remembered.

CHAPTER 3

THE MYSTERY BEGINS

Meow, meow.

The purring of a cat was the first thing I heard, and then I felt the soft tap of a paw on my face, jostling me awake.

"Where am I?" I said out loud, not expecting an answer but hoping it would all come back to me.

I took in a deep breath, trying to figure out just where I was. The feel of the cold floor on my face sent a big shiver up my spine. The side of my face felt sore and bruised, and when I raised my hand up, I felt a small bump just above my right ear. Ouch! The memory of what had happened slowly came back to me; the last thing I remembered was saying good-bye to Mrs. Pickens, walking into the den, and tripping over something that hadn't been there yesterday. How was I going to explain this new bruise to Allymom? There would be questions. I just knew it.

Trying to figure out just where I was in the room, I sat up and knelt on the floor as I searched in front of me with my hands, trying to touch something that would guide me, that would help me figure out where I was in the room. I had lost all sense of direction. With my arms extended, I grasped at the air like an octopus, moving about on my knees, until I felt the hard wood of a chair leg. This gave me the guidance I needed to know where

I was, since the chair was always on the right side when I walked into the den.

As I inched along on the floor, still on my knees, my hands were out in front of me, serving as my "guide dogs." My left hand immediately came into contact with something cold and hard, like ice-cold metal. It felt as cold as the wind in a Buffalo snowstorm. I quickly pulled back my hand as if I'd been burned, my breaths coming faster and faster.

"Calm yourself down, Ethan," I said out loud, and I took a slow, deep breath. As my curiosity got the best of me, I slowly reached out to touch it again.

I picked up the newfound object, trying to figure out just what I was holding. It felt strange yet somehow familiar in my hands, like an odd pair of glasses but heavier—no, more like goggles, goggles like the ones Sergeant Bailey had told me about from when he was in Vietnam, the ones with night vision. What I held now reminded me of the goggles he had brought to school one day and let me feel as he described them; he had let me put them on, even though I couldn't see. Without even thinking, I put these on, and that's when it happened. It was magical. It was distorted but exciting—blurry, I guess those with sight would say, or what I thought blurry was. At first, I couldn't believe my eyes— yes, my *eyes*—but as the picture in front of me slowly became clearer, my mouth dried up, and I could barely swallow. I opened my mouth to yell, but nothing came out but a small gasp. I was nearly speechless.

"I can see," I whispered, afraid that someone would hear me. "I think I can see. I think I can see."

Was this vision? Was this what it was like to "see"? Yes, I had vision, but it was not what I had thought it would be like. It was more like what I had heard 3-D was like, like in all those movies that I had never been able to watch, like *Shrek* and *Toy Story*. I sat there for what seemed like forever, just sat there with these strange goggles on and the biggest smile ever on my face.

As I turned my head to the right, my whole body began to shake. What was that? I moved my head again, and what I was looking at moved in sync with me. Was that me? I moved, and it moved. I moved my hand up to my face, and it moved too. Was that my reflection looking back at me? Was I looking into a mirror? I remembered that Mrs. Pickens had talked about her antique mirror, large and ornate, sitting on the floor in the den. A family heirloom, she had said. I just sat there and stared. This was little old me! This was Ethan Pero, supersleuth, looking back at me! There was no stopping the smile that was growing on my face. Yes, my face.

I heard the meow of Mrs. Pickens's cat again and turned my head. The cat had her head cocked sideways. She was hesitant to come closer to me, but as she did, I reached out to touch her. She was a beauty, just as I knew she would be. Her soft purr let me know she was happy, and we sat there, just the two of us, both in the moment, this super-duper moment.

"Katy-do-do, Katy-do-do." I said her name over and over as I petted her soft fur, and she rubbed her head on me. She meowed a few more times, and it made me feel like she was saying my name back to me: "Ethan, Ethan, Ethan." She opened and closed what I knew were her eyes, slowly. She was blinking, I guess. I have heard that's what cats do when they love you. It was like she knew I could finally see her. She rubbed her head on my pant leg as I continued to pet her. I felt like I was purring too.

I turned back to look at my reflection. I guess I had never thought about what I looked like. I had never asked anyone what the color of my hair was, whether I had freckles, or whether I had a nice smile. Actually, without sight, I had never known the questions to ask. I guess they were details that had never mattered to me before or that I hadn't even cared about.

But now I was transfixed on my image, and all I could do was smile at myself. I brought my hand to my face and traced it with my fingers. I felt the soreness and raised bruise on the side of my face, a gentle reminder: a souvenir of my recent fall. I watched myself in the mirror as if I were a mime.

"Hello, Ethan," I said and laughed, not a giggle but one of those hearty laughs, the kind that can bring tears to your eyes. I snorted through my nose, and when I stopped, I felt so good inside. I felt like I had taken first prize in the school's spelling bee.

Caught up in all that was happening to me, the vision and all, I didn't realize until just then that the bookcase seemed to have shifted from where I knew it always was in the room. From where I was sitting, it should have been a hand's reach from me, but it was much farther away. It had shifted far left of its usual position along the wall, and in its place was a large dark opening, like what I thought the entrance to a black hole or the opening to a bear cave would be like. This was all so new to me; I really didn't know what I was looking at.

The goggles seemingly sensed that I needed to see more and emitted a glow—a light, I guess—that allowed me to see deeper into this area. Did the goggles know what I was thinking? I got the immediate feeling that my thoughts were somehow linked to the goggles. Wow, these goggles rocked!

This was all such a mystery to me, but it was what I had been waiting for all my life. I knew it was just the start of something different and exciting. My stomach flip-flopped with the building excitement, and I swallowed a couple of times, afraid I would barf all over the floor. *Ethan, get a grip,* I thought. I stood up quickly and then slowly walked toward the bookcase; it felt as if it were a mile away, but actually, it was just a couple of steps more than usual. I steadied myself as well as my nerves by putting both hands on the top shelf of the bookcase and leaned over to the right to peer into the deep, dark hole. I felt a nervous energy building inside me, a mixture of fear and excitement.

It looked really dark in there but comforting because it was just like my blind world, since I could see nothing in front of me. Standing there on wobbly legs, I moved forward, taking small steps and bending down low to get into what seemed like a tunnel. The goggles again adjusted to the change in light. A soft pounding echoed in my ears as I felt my heart beating hard in my chest. The feeling reminded me of how Addison had told me she felt when riding the Comet at Crystal Beach, one of the largest roller coasters in our area. The thrill of it all was just beginning, and as I slowly made my way into the tunnel, I sensed that it was going to be a heck of a ride.

CHAPTER 4

THE CAVERNOUS HOLE

Continuing to walk deeper into the cavernous hole, I reached a larger opening. *This must be what it would feel like to walk into the mouth of a large whale,* I thought. I felt like I was being swallowed up as I made my way into the belly of the cave. It smelled a lot like school—musty and damp but even worse than the school smelled. Pee-yew!

All sorts of instrument-like paraphernalia that I didn't recognize lined the walls of the room. Standing there in silence, my hands tingling and dripping with sweat, I swallowed hard, not knowing whether to be scared or excited.

"Ethan," said a robotic voice. "Ethan."

I turned around quickly to see who was calling my name. But spinning in a circle, I saw nothing, no one. "Who are you?" I said in a nervous whisper, barely able to get the words out of my mouth.

My eyes widened, and my jaw dropped as it spoke my name again, and I realized the voice was coming from the goggles. A picture then appeared in the right lens of the goggles. "Table," the voice said.

Were these goggles identifying the objects I needed to recognize? There before me was a table, an exact replica of the one the goggles had shown me. How cool was this? The goggles were teaching me!

"Book," it said next, showing me another picture.

I picked up a small book that was sitting on the table. It was held closed by some sort of string.

"Lariat, a leather piece of string used to secure things," the voice continued as it showed me a picture of the leather string.

I had a feeling as I turned the book over in my hands that it held information that was somehow meant for me to find—sightless, little me. The book's cover had a picture of the goggles on it, exactly like the ones I was now wearing. *This is my destiny,* I thought. It all felt like a dream, and I pinched myself to see if I would wake up. "Ouch!" I said out loud. "This is definitely not a dream."

Placing the book back on the table, I picked up one of the instruments. It was square with pointed edges, and it felt heavy and cold. Struggling not to drop it, I held it tight with both hands. It had a bunch of dials and buttons on it, much like the goggles.

"Voice recorder," the monotone voice of the goggles uttered. "Push red button." A picture showed up in my goggles, showing me exactly what to do next.

I pushed the red button, and I heard a man's voice, deep and gruff. It sounded oddly familiar, and I immediately thought of Mr. Goodsmith.

"Greetings and welcome. Your life is about to change in ways you never expected. Take the leather book with you. It is yours for getting this far. Start reading it, and you will have a better understanding of what is in store for you. You will learn the history of the goggles and all that you find here."

I grabbed the book and held it tight against my chest. I decided I would put it in my backpack, where it would be safe. Allymom always said her father, my Grandpa Al, used to say, "You never realize how your life can change in one day until it does." I finally understood the meaning of those words as my heart beat like a drum underneath my jacket; it felt like my heart was doing jumping jacks inside my chest, trying to make a quick escape.

The muffled sound of a slamming door brought me back to reality, and I heard Mrs. Pickens singing. "If I had a hammer, I'd hammer in the morning ..."

Moving quickly, I made my way out of this newfound place, and as I did, a strange feeling came over me, as if someone or something was watching me. The hairs on the back of my neck stood up as if a cold wind had passed by me. It was just a feeling, a sense of something. A soft, whispering sound reached my ears, but looking back, I saw nothing. The bookcase slid to the right, back into its original place, at the same time that I took my last step out of the cave, stepped back into the den, and removed the goggles, going back to my world of darkness. Was it just a coincidence that the cave closed when I took the goggles off? Or just plain weird?

The *thunk, thunk, thunk* of heavy footsteps on the wooden floor told me that Mrs. Pickens was close as I sat down on the sofa. The soft meow of Katy-do-do helped to calm my nerves. As she rubbed her head on me, I petted her with one hand and tried to cover the bruise on the side of my face with my hair, since I didn't want to alert anyone to anything unusual. I moved quickly to put the goggles and the book in my backpack and then reached for the snack that Mrs. Pickens always left for me on the table. I took a bite; it was sweet and chocolaty. I could feel my heart rate slowing with each nibble of the snack.

"What's the story, morning glory?" Mrs. Pickens said happily, the smells of talcum powder and baby lotion clouding the air. That was Mrs. Pickens for you, forever singing or quoting some quirky saying or repeating lines from a classic novel.

"Just having a snack, Mrs. P., and working on my homework. There's a show on audiotape I'm planning on listening to when I get home, and if my homework's not done, you know what Allymom will say. Did you have this much homework when you went to school, Mrs. Pickens?"

"Homework is good for you, Ethan. It's like a workout for the brain—builds brain cells and makes you smarter, and that's a good thing, right? How was the snack today?" she asked, her voice hopeful.

"Mmm, mmm, Mrs. Pickens. I think it was your best one yet." Sometimes I had to be careful about how I responded to that question, especially when the snack wasn't so good, so that she wouldn't try to give me more.

"Well, okeydokey, artichokey," she said cheerily.

"Guess I'll be heading home, Mrs. P. It's just about that time." I pushed the button on my watch and heard the audible time. Allymom would be home soon.

Grabbing my backpack, I made my way to the back door. It took all my inner strength not to blurt out to her what had happened before she got home. As the screen door slammed shut, I heard Mrs. Pickens's muffled good-bye.

I reached the back door of my house in no time and used the coded Braille entry keypad to unlock the door. It was a secret code that Allymom had let me choose—the entrance to my own Batcave. As I walked in, the phone was ringing. I knew who it was.

As soon as I picked up the phone, I said with a laugh, "I'm home safe and sound, Mrs. P."

"Peace out, cub scout." And the phone line went dead.

A moment later, there was a distinctive knock at the back door. *Tap ... tap ... tap-tap ... tap.*

I opened the door without hesitation, recognizing Addison's secret coded knock. We had come up with this because Allymom's number-one rule when I was home alone was "Never open a door to a stranger." There sure were a lot of rules growing up.

"Hey, Ethan," Addison said. Her voice made my heart skip a beat, and my hands started to sweat. If I were a superhero, Addison would definitely be Lois Lane to my Superman.

I didn't know what Addison looked like, but I didn't have to; I knew she was perfect. Being blind, I was never able to judge people on what they looked like, what color their hair or eyes were, or how they looked in skinny jeans. Actually, I didn't even know what skinny jeans were. Mr. Goodsmith always said, "You judge people by the content of their words and their actions, not by how they look." I guess that made it easier for me than for others to not let how Addison looked interfere with my opinion of her. I didn't have a choice, so it was a no-brainer.

"Addison, what's up? How ya f-feeling?" I said, slightly stuttering. Now I was beginning to sound like Mikey. I could smell the sweet scent of strawberries whenever she was around.

"My little brother's been sick, coughing and sneezing all over me. I woke with the sniffles this morning, so my mom kept me home, but I feel better now. I'll pick you up for school tomorrow, like always."

"Great," I said. I swear I could never think of anything to say to Addison when she was around. Nothing witty. Mrs. Pickens called it being "tongue-tied." I wasn't sure that was actually possible, but it sure made a lot of sense. Telling her about the goggles would have to wait for now, but if I told anyone, it would be Addison. She always had my back, and I knew she could keep a secret.

"Okay then. See you in the morning, Ethan."

"K," I said and closed the back door.

I flew up to my room: twenty steps up the stairs, a right turn, and ten more steps to my bedroom door. I felt like I had wings.

I locked my bedroom door behind me and reached for the goggles. Moving quickly to my bedroom window, I hoped to catch a quick glimpse of Addison.

"Addison Meloy," the voice confirmed. "Five feet tall, dark brown hair, and blue eyes."

So that's what blue eyes look like, I thought as the goggles somehow knew to zoom in on Addison's eyes. I couldn't take my eyes off her. I followed her every move with the goggles as she made her way down the street to her house until she disappeared inside.

Watching her left me speechless, and I moved to the bed and sat down, lost in my thoughts about all that had happened today. My future was unfolding before me, and I was excited to begin this unknown journey. I smiled to myself, knowing I would have Lois Lane at my side.

CHAPTER 5

GOGGLES CAN BE GREAT

Kicking off my sneakers, I lay back on my bed, and my head sank into my pillow. Looking upward at the bare ceiling, I could feel excitement building inside me. I was a runaway locomotive on the tracks, gaining speed and momentum. I was a blank slate, as blank as the ceiling, and as a new chapter in my life was about to begin, I realized I had the tools that would help me write my future. I grabbed the book I had found at Mrs. Pickens's house from my backpack, hoping that the voice would help me retrieve the information the book held.

"Hey, P-Pero, what-ch-cha d-doing?" Mikey's voice came slithering to me from the open window in my room.

I made my way over to the window, still wearing the goggles, and saw a boy standing down below.

"Mikey McGurren," said the voice.

I squinted a bit, and the glasses automatically zoomed in on his face. *What are those little dots all over his face?* I thought.

"Freckles," the voice said and then continued to describe Mikey to me in detail. "Five-five, 109 pounds, red hair, blue eyes."

For some reason, I didn't get the same feeling from seeing Mikey's blue eyes up close that I did from seeing Addison's as the goggles zoomed in on Mikey's face.

Mikey stood there, waiting for me to answer him.

"Homework, of course," I answered.

"Hey, what are those g-goggles you're wearing, P-Pero?" Mikey stammered up to me.

"Oh, just something I found. Ya like 'em?"

"Yeah, yeah, they l-look s-super s-strange."

"They are." With that, I closed the window, turned my back on him, and walked back to my bed, smiling to myself. *Take that, McGurren,* I thought.

"Be p-prepared, P-Pero. Be very p-prepared," called Mikey, his voice muffled through the closed window. He made a fake, evil-sounding laughing noise.

For some reason, his threat didn't bother me. I knew these goggles would somehow protect me. I felt invincible, and little did Mikey know how prepared I was. Reaching for the book again, I turned to the first page. My finger landed on the first word by accident, and I heard the voice.

"This."

I took my finger off the page and placed it back on the same word.

The voice responded again: "This."

As I moved my pointer finger along the words on the page, the voice continued to read the sentence to me.

"This book will change your life in ways that you never knew possible."

Oh, wow, I thought, *LeapFrog has nothing on this.*

The voice continued, "This book will guide and teach you the basic instructions on the use of goggles."

Just below these words was a picture of the goggles I had found. Each part was labeled, and as I touched the various words, the goggles taught me the function of each dial and button through words and pictures that showed up in the right eye of my goggles.

I got through several chapters before I heard the closing of the front door.

"I'm home, Ethan!" Allymom yelled to me from downstairs. "Supper in thirty minutes."

"Be right down, Allymom. I'm starving."

I put everything away in my backpack and shoved it under my bed, excited and eager to get back to it as soon as I could.

I flew downstairs in a supersleuth fashion, no cape required, knowing the book would have to wait for now.

CHAPTER 6

BIKE THEFTS

As I made my way into the kitchen, the clanging of pots and pans alerted me that Allymom had already started to get dinner ready. She was a whiz in the kitchen and could have a great dinner on the table in thirty minutes or less. The TV chefs had nothing on her.

I knew where just about everything was in our home. Allymom didn't move things around like Mrs. Pickens did, so I made my way to the kitchen table easily and sat down in my chair. Before Allymom even spoke, I knew what she was going to say.

"So, Ethan, I received a call from Principal Robertson today. Can you tell me about that?"

Am I psychic or what? I thought. "Well, you see, um, I kind of fell into Mikey this morning. I tripped over something just after I walked through the school doors, and that something happened to be Mikey. We both wound up in Principal Robertson's office, but it all seemed to work out okay, and to be honest, this time, I don't think Mikey set me up for the fall." My explanation of the rest of the story seemed to satisfy her concern.

"Okay, Ethan. Can we just have one week where you don't end up in the principal's office?" I opened my mouth to speak, but she interrupted me. "Ethan, let's just eat. I had a crazy day at work, and you confirmed what Principal Robertson told me, so it's all good." I heard her set my plate in front of me. "Pasta at three o'clock, peas at six, garlic bread at nine."

I dug into the food quickly, happy that there would be no more questions about the school incident.

"Ethan, there've been a bunch of bicycle thefts in the area lately. Have you heard anything at school about that? Several police reports have been made, and the police are stumped, since there are no witnesses. It's a real mystery—something I know you of all people would be interested in."

Working as a reporter, Allymom always had interesting subjects to talk about during dinner. She was well known in the news-reporting business as a "tough as nails" journalist, and her job always sounded exciting to me.

"Haven't heard a thing, but I'll keep my eyes and ears open— well, at least my ears," I said with a smile.

"Oh my, my, my, what shall I do with you?" Allymom said, and I could tell she was smiling too.

"Guess you're stuck with me," I said back to her.

Allymom became my mother after my birth parents died. My real mom, Allymom's sister, passed away when I was born, and my dad died shortly after. But it is all good in my mind and is not something I have dwelled on. Her name is Allison, and I just stuck the two words together when I was little: Allymom. She is all I've really ever known, and to be honest, I couldn't have chosen a better mom if I had been given the choice myself.

"So, Allymom, what do you know so far about the missing bikes?" I asked.

"Well, nothing really so far. It's not one particular type of bike that has gone missing; there have been girls' bikes, boys' bikes, and tricycles, and the thief isn't targeting any particular color or style. We haven't got wind of anyone selling any bikes either, which adds to the mystery around this whole thing. They just kind of disappear at all times of the day and night."

"I'll have to ask Addison in the morning if she's heard anything, and I'll ask Sergeant Bailey too. If anyone knows anything about it, it would be him. Well, I guess it's back to my homework, and then I'm hoping to catch a few minutes of that new superhero movie on the audio disc that I got from the library."

We finished dinner, and I put my dirty dishes on the counter. Allymom would do the rest. Allymom gave me a kiss on the forehead, as always. She said her mom had always done that when she was little. Allymom was like that; she liked tradition.

"Don't forget to wash your face and hands and brush and floss, Ethan," she said, knowing I sometimes get so wrapped up in things that I forget to do my nightly routine.

"Okay," I said with a groan.

I made my way back up to my room, thinking, *Missing bikes, missing bikes.* My heart started to beat faster, and I thought about the goggles. I couldn't wait to get back to my room and put them on. Allymom was right; this could be just what I was looking for. I felt a mystery was right before me, and I was going to be the supersleuth who would solve it—well, with a little help, of course.

CHAPTER 7

SHH ... IT'S A SECRET

As I landed on my bed in my room face-first on the covers, a laugh started to build inside me. I felt like a balloon that was filled with too much air and ready to pop. That nervous energy was building inside me again. It felt like the low hum of a cat purring and then quickly built to the idling of a fast race car on the dragway. I didn't know if I would even be able to fall asleep that night. I was so preoccupied with my thoughts that I didn't hear Allymom's footsteps approaching.

"What's all that giggling about?" I heard her say.

My laugh came to an abrupt halt. I think I actually inhaled some saliva into my lungs. I started to cough and hack and was speechless. *Ethan, get your act together to avoid all suspicion,* I said to myself. I needed time to think about what I was going to tell Allymom. I didn't like keeping secrets from her. We shared everything, and I wanted to share this with her, just not now. It would have to wait.

"Nothing really. I was just thinking about other things that happened today, at school and after school." I did some quick thinking. "During the morning announcements at school, they talked about looking toward your future, setting goals for yourself, and being part of the changes in your life, not just waiting for life to intervene. So I think things are going to change for me."

"Well, good," Allymom said wistfully. "Life does travel at its own pace, and you just can't let it go by too quickly. You'll see; you'll be my age before you know it, with all the drama it has to offer."

Drama, I thought. *If she only knew.*

"Okay, Ethan, not too late tonight. In bed by nine."

I heard her hit the button on my audio clock. The friendly clock lady's voice let me know it was 7:30 p.m., so I had plenty of time before bed—plenty of time to read, finish up my homework, and even possibly watch that video I wanted to see.

As I heard the sounds of Allymom walking away, I got up and closed the door of my room, as secrecy at this time was my top priority. I reached under the bed for my backpack, took the goggles out, and put them on again. I would need a better hiding place for them and the book. I didn't know if I should keep them both with me all the time, but I didn't want to let them out of my sight, if you know what I mean.

Where to put them? I went to my laptop and turned it on. It had an audio function for me, but with the goggles, I didn't really need that. The laptop had a Braille keyboard, and Allymom said I could type faster than she did. I typed "holders for goggles" into the search engine. All sorts of things popped up on the screen in front of me. This was all so new but, at the same time, exciting. As I put my finger on the screen, the voice from the goggles identified everything, just as it had with the book. What could these goggles not do?

I went on a lot of different websites, including Google, Amazon, and eBay. These were all websites I had heard people talking about, but I had never used them before. I audio-commanded my computer to go to a manga website, hoping I would find some cool holder there. I had manga and Pokémon audiobooks, but actually seeing all those characters, with my own eyes, was way beyond cool. The colors exploded on the screen in front of me, but nothing I saw seemed right for a holder for my goggles.

Out of the corner of my eye, on my bookshelf, I saw it. It was perfect, with room enough for the small leather book and the goggles too. Why hadn't I thought about it before? I could leave it out in the open, just like I had always done; no one would think twice about it. I got up from my computer chair and went to retrieve it. I stopped and stared at it for a while, and it made me think of my dad. Maybe this was his way of letting me know he was thinking of me too. I grabbed it off the shelf and went back to sit on my bed.

"Binocular case," said the goggles' voice. I smiled because I didn't need anyone to identify this item. I had made my own mental picture in my mind years ago, from holding and touching it over and over.

My dad's binocular case was the perfect camouflage for the goggles. Allymom had told me Dad was an avid bird-watcher, and he had always carried the binoculars and the case with him wherever he went. Allymom told me my dad could identify any bird by sight or sound. I put the goggles in the case, and they fit perfectly, like it was meant to be, and the book slid easily into the inside flap, like the case was meant for it too. Everything seemed to be falling into place. This whole saga felt like a big jigsaw puzzle, each piece having its place, and I, Ethan Pero, was at the center of the puzzle, the star, the main character, the supersleuth. The future, I knew, was going to be filled with things I had never even dreamed would happen to me. It was just like the morning announcements had said that day: "Concentrate and focus on what you want, and you will see your dreams come true. Be in the driver's seat of your future and your own destiny."

"Look out, future," I said out loud. "I'm a-coming!"

CHAPTER 8

WHO KNEW ROUTINE COULD CHANGE?

Remembering Allymom's words, I went into the bathroom to do my nightly routine before going to bed. Even things as boring as washing my face and brushing my teeth felt new to me. I smiled the whole time as I watched myself in the mirror. My movements were strange to watch. It felt like I was watching someone else's life, like it was a video, and I was playing the starring role. It was just plain weird. Yeah, that's what it was—weird. It was hard to believe that the person looking back at me in the mirror was me!

Changing out of my school clothes, I grabbed my T-shirt and Superman sweatpants from where I had left them that morning on the bathroom counter and quickly changed into them. There was no doubt I was as quick as Clark Kent when he changed into his alter ego. I caught my reflection in the mirror again and did my superhero pose.

As I posed, I heard a woof on the other side of the closed bathroom door. Opening the door, I saw Tucker standing there, his head slanted to one side as he looked at me, his wagging tail hitting the door like a flyswatter.

"What? You don't recognize a supersleuth when you see one?" I said to him, almost hoping for a response.

"Dog, Lhasa apso, purebred, brown-black in color, age approximately nine to ten years old, sixty-three to seventy in human years," said the goggles.

Tucker continued his whimper and wagged his tail some more, licking the top of my foot. Yuck! I reached down to touch his soft fur with my hand, and my petting him made his tail wag even more. *Dogs are so easy to please,* I thought as he followed me out of the bathroom, his nails *click-clacking* on the tile floor behind me.

Sitting on my bed, I put the goggles under my pillow for safekeeping while I slept; I wanted them close to me. I *needed* them to be close to me. I was almost afraid I would wake up and find it all had been a dream. I touched them again, and the metal was cold on my fingers. It was strange that something so cold to the touch could make me feel so warm inside.

I hadn't realized how tired I was until just then, and reading more of the book or even watching some of the video would have to wait. My eyelids felt heavy, and I didn't think I could keep my eyes open for too much longer. I hadn't realized how much using your eyes could wear a person out, but I wasn't complaining. Tucker hopped up on my bed and nestled next to my feet, his usual sleeping place.

"Night, Tucker, old boy." Feeling myself drifting off to sleep, I wondered how I would find the right words to tell Addison about the goggles. I knew that I would because I wanted her to be a part of this with me. I just didn't know how to start the conversation. I guessed that just blurting it out would be the best way to go, but then another idea came to mind, and I knew I had found the perfect way to tell her. Tomorrow couldn't come soon enough.

CHAPTER 9

A NEW DAY

The voice from my audible alarm clock woke me up. It was morning, and I felt rested and ready to start a new day. The sound of Tucker barking downstairs and the smell of Allymom's coffee brewing told me that I was the last one to get up.

Panic quickly set in as I felt under my pillow, searching for my goggles, and did not find them. I bolted upright, lifting the pillow as I did, and felt my heart start to beat faster. I felt all around my bed and then lifted my quilt, shaking it out and hoping to hear or feel something. Had it all been just a dream? My heart sank as I quickly got out of bed, tripping on the rug. As cold metal touched my foot, I realized the goggles must have fallen off the bed during the night.

I made a mental note: *Put the goggles back in the case when you aren't using them.*

"You up, Ethan?" Allymom yelled from downstairs. "Breakfast is just about done. Scrambled or poached today?"

"Your choice," I said. I felt the day was going to be filled with a lot of decisions, and one less that I had to think about would make my day that much easier.

I used the bathroom and hit my audible time clock before heading downstairs. "Six forty-five."

I didn't have to leave the house until seven thirty, so I had plenty of time. I dressed quickly because wearing the goggles made everything so much easier. The voice of the goggles identified things for me, in a way educating me about a world with vision.

"Blue shirt, tan pants, white-blue Nikes, underwear, and socks." This was all so new and definitely something I could get used to. Never again would I go to school wearing an outfit of plaid and stripes or hear the whispers of the other kids at school commenting on what I was wearing.

I grabbed my backpack and the binocular case and made my way downstairs. Just as I was about to round the corner to the kitchen, I saw my reflection in the glass of the china cabinet and realized I was still wearing the goggles. Luckily, the voice was silent; my secret was still safe. Taking them off, I put them in the case, walked into the kitchen, and sat down at the table.

"Yes, sir. I am going to get right on with that missing bicycles story," Allymom said.

I figured Allymom was on the phone, since I didn't hear anyone else talking.

"No, sir, no leads to date, but I've put some feelers out, and I hope to get some more answers today. And yes, I will be stopping by the police department this morning. I'll check in with you when I get in. Bye for now." I heard Allymom hang up the phone, and then heard her footsteps getting closer to where I was sitting.

"How'd you sleep, Ethan? I swear I heard you talking in your sleep, tossing and turning, saying something about goggles."

"Uh ... uh ... actually, I slept like a bear in hibernation ... *grrr.*" I attempted a bear growl, hoping to quickly change the subject, and heard Allymom start to laugh.

"Oh, Ethan, you do have an imagination. Eat up. Addison's mom called and said she will be back at school today and will be picking you up as usual this morning."

"So who was that you were talking to?" I asked, hoping to get some information.

"That was Big Lou, my editor. He wants me to stay on top of this missing bike saga because it's starting to gain momentum in the area, and he wants the *Tribune* to have the lead story."

"Hmm, it sounds like a big mystery is developing. Keep me posted, Allymom. I want to hear all the clues. Maybe I can help solve it too."

"Okay, my little superhero, but eat your breakfast before it gets cold so you'll have the strength for all your detective work," Allymom said while ruffling up my hair.

If only you knew. I gobbled the eggs up in no time. Done with breakfast, I made my way back upstairs to grab the last of my things I would need for school. Addison would be here right on time to walk with me, and she hated being late. With the goggles safe in the binocular case and the book safe in the inside compartment, I put the whole thing in my backpack, secured the small lock on the zippered latch, and placed the key on a chain to hang around my neck.

Hearing voices in the kitchen, I realized Addison was here and talking to Allymom in the kitchen. Lacing up my Nikes, I headed back downstairs.

"I know, Miss Pero," Addison said to Allymom. "He sure can eat a lot."

"Hey now, you two. I'm right here," I said with a smirk on my face. "Don't they say that growing boys have big appetites?"

"You have an appetite for two growing boys, Ethan," Allymom said jokingly.

"Well, let's hit the road, Addison," I said before she could, since she was always telling me how slow and unorganized I was.

I heard the screen door screech slowly open and knew that Addison was holding it open for me. It was kind of a role reversal, but we both knew that was all right as we headed down the street, side by side.

"Addison, I have something really important to tell you," I said as we continued walking.

CHAPTER 10

THE TALE CONTINUES

"What is it, Ethan? It sounds important."

Walking to school was usually just part of my boring routine, but this morning was different as I searched for the right words to tell Addison my secret. The cool breeze made my ears feel cold, so I pulled my sweatshirt closer around my head.

"Addison, did you ever have a secret so big it was hard to find the right words to tell someone about it?"

The whir of a bike swept past us and interrupted our conversation. The familiar ring of the bike bell alerted me to who it was.

"Yo, Ethan and Addie," Tony S. said in his New Jersey accent.

"Yo," Addison and I said in unison.

"That is so strange," Addison said. "Tony S. isn't riding his usual bike. This one is blue with red fenders, and he's hauling another one behind him. I don't think I've ever seen him do that before."

"Hmm, that is strange," I said to Addison, while thinking, *Missing-bike strange.* "You know, Addison, a slew of bikes have gone missing in the area. You don't think ... no, couldn't be," I said, my mind taking off in a thousand directions.

"No, not Tony S.," Addison said. "He would never, would he? You know, we really don't know him that well. No, couldn't be."

"I suppose you're right," I said, not sure whether I actually believed what I had just said. "Allymom is even writing a story on it, so you know it must be big."

"I guess so ... So, Ethan, what is this big secret you have to tell me?" Addison asked.

The loud jangling of wind chimes interrupted our conversation again, and I knew we were approaching Mr. Goodsmith's house. School was close; a few hundred steps after his house were the school gates. This was my life—steps and smells. That sounded like the name of a song that would play on Nash FM, the local country music station.

We kept on walking, and the chimes faded into the distance as we approached the school. The voices of the kids greeted us, as usual, as everyone waited for the first bell to ring, which would give us about five minutes to get to homeroom and be in our assigned seats on time.

There seemed to be a lot of chatter this morning as we stood outside, waiting to go in—more than the usual goings-on—but lately, things were far from the usual. I heard bits and pieces of conversations as we stood there waiting.

"Yeah, Bobby's bike got stolen last week."

"Two bikes missing Monday, two more on Tuesday."

"J-Jimmy got his b-bike s-stolen from the l-library. H-he forgot to c-chain it up, and his m-mom is r-really m-mad. That was a n-new I-IZIP. He's g-grounded for t-two whole w-weeks." I recognized Mikey's voice as the breeze brought the faint smell of onion to my nose. Yuck!

"Addie, did I hear Mikey right?" I said eagerly. The mystery was about to get exciting, and I could barely say the words.

"Yeah, Ethan, I guess you were right about what's going on with the bikes around here. I hope my bike is okay at my house. I forgot to put the chain on it and lock it to the fence. My dad will be really mad if it gets taken, and I don't even want to think about what my mom will say."

"Something strange is happening in this town." My thoughts drifted back to the goggles. "I guess I'm going to keep you hanging a while longer on what I have to tell you. It can wait till after school," I said, trying to keep calm as I spoke. I knew I had to keep my cool—"Cool as a cucumber," as Mrs. Pickens always said.

We both entered the building with Sergeant Bailey's voice greeting everyone as we walked through the school doors.

"Morning, Mr. Ethan," Sergeant Bailey said gruffly. "Let's have a good day today, you hear?"

"Yes, sir," I replied, giving him my one-hand salute while touching my other hand to the backpack where the goggles were hidden. Yes, my secret would have to wait for now, I thought, as we made our way to our first classroom and morning announcements.

CHAPTER 11

TRYING TO TELL ADDIE

"See you at lunch, Ethan," Addison whispered into my ear as she left me at the door of my homeroom. "And I want to hear all about that big secret of yours."

I waited in the doorway as she walked away, heading to her homeroom, until I couldn't hear her footsteps any longer. Now I had an image to go along with all those footsteps. Now I had an image to go along with the voice and that sweet strawberry smell that always lingered long after she walked away. Addison and I were in some classes together, but I was unlucky enough to have Mikey in homeroom.

"Coming in, Ethan, or are you going to stand in the hall today?" Miss Ulrich, my homeroom teacher, said.

"Nope, coming in, Miss Ulrich." Reaching for the first desk, I began the count in my head. *One ... two ... three ... four.* I then turned right, walked straight ahead, and began again. *One ... two.*

That was my desk—four across and two down—in all my classes, which made things easier for me. By the smell of things, I could tell Mikey was in his assigned seat directly behind me. Sometimes life gives you a one-two punch—in this case, Mikey and the way he smelled. But sometimes, as Mrs. Pickens said, life could bring you roses. Addison was roses.

"P-Pero, P-Pero, you're my h-hero!" Mikey said in a mockingly girlish voice.

I thought about the goggles—little did he know he might be eating those words really soon—and stayed silent. I had learned that my saying little or nothing irritated Mikey more than if I said anything back to him. It was the little game we played. Kind of like cat and mouse or Tom and Jerry.

"Okay, Michael, let's not start so early in the morning. Everyone, take your assigned seats, and wait for the morning announcements from Principal Robertson," Miss Ulrich said. I liked Miss Ulrich. She kept Mikey in line for me, and anything that helped me out with Mikey was good in my book.

Attendance was taken, and then the loud, booming voice of Principal Robertson echoed from overhead as he started morning announcements through the PA system.

"Children, the Tonawanda police have notified us about some missing bikes in the area. Let's remember all our bike safety rules, mainly locking your bikes securely in the bike zone by the playground. Sergeant Bailey will be adding some increased security details in this area, and all students must abide by these rules. Okay, then, let's have a great day."

The chatter started again in the classroom as some kids left to go to their first class. Mine was here, so I stayed in my seat. Hearing the chair behind me slide across the floor, I knew Mikey had got up to go to his next class, and right on cue, he kicked my seat as he walked by me. I sat there unmoving, like a statue.

"Later, P-Pero," he said as he walked away. I continued my silence, not wanting to give him a reason to say more. Allymom was right: sometimes, the less you say, the better off you are. Ah, that mom wisdom again. I had to admit sometimes it came in handy.

Miss Ulrich started her lecture, and then the morning just seemed to fly by as I made my way to my next few classes. As soon as a class began, it seemed like the bell rang, telling me that it was time to leave and head to my next one. It was hard for me to keep focused on what the teachers were saying because my thoughts kept drifting to the goggles, the book, and the missing bikes.

When the bell rang for lunch at the end of my fourth-period math class, my teacher, Mr. Bleyle, led me to the door, and Addison was there to help me get to the cafeteria.

"I'm starving, Addison. They better have something good to eat."

"Ethan, whatever it is, you'll eat it, I have no doubt. If there's one thing you're not, you're definitely not picky when it comes to food."

We both laughed because she was right about that. We continued to the cafeteria, grabbed a tray, and got in the lunch line.

"What'll it be today, young man?" I recognized the voice of Jessie, who worked in the kitchen and served our lunch to us.

"You do the picking for me, Mr. Jessie. You've never steered me wrong yet."

"Okay, will do. Cheeseburger—ketchup and pickles only, if I recall—side salad, Italian dressing, and an apple for dessert. How's that sound, young man?"

"Sounds great," I replied.

Addison got her food and then steered me to our usual table, trays in hand. We sat with the same kids every day, our own little "lunch bunch."

"Hey, you two," Laura said. Laura lived next door to Addison, and she was in my English class.

"Hey back," Addison and I said at the same time. We did that a lot, it seemed. Allymom said sometimes we were like an old married couple. I wasn't sure what she meant by that.

"What did everyone think about the morning announcements and all those bikes going missing?" I said, hoping to get some new intel.

"Well ... I heard that even the cops don't know what's going on, but the numbers are adding up," Brian Geary said. Brian and I had been friends since kindergarten. It was always Mikey, Brian, and me. Even Brian couldn't put a finger on how things had gone wrong with Mikey.

"Allymom is working on the story for the *Tribune*. There are a lot of unsolved issues and loose ends," I said, raising my eyebrows for emphasis.

"Ooh, gotta love a mystery, huh, Ethan?" Laura said, knowing my love for the unsolved mysteries in life.

"Okay, kids, stop your talking, and eat up; lunch is over in ten minutes," said Mrs. D., the lunch lady.

"Yes, Mrs. D," everyone at the table said in unison. We all laughed and then finished eating. When done, we put our trays away and headed out of the cafeteria.

Between classes at our lockers, the chatter again was about the missing bikes, and I couldn't wait to get back to the book and my goggles.

Luckily for me, the rest of the school day sped by, and before I knew it, the bell announcing our freedom was ringing. Sergeant Bailey led me out the back door and into the fresh air.

Addison was in the same place she always was, waiting to the left of the school doors, ready to walk home with me. "Boy, Ethan, you're raring to go. The Green Lantern has nothing on you."

"Just have a lot on my mind lately," I said.

"Oh yeah? Like what? Does this have anything to do with what you wanted to tell me?" Addison said, sounding eager to hear what might be happening. Like me, she loved an adventure or a mystery. She was always reading the latest mystery novel. Sometimes she even read it out loud to me.

"Wouldn't you like to know?" I whispered, hoping it sounded all the more mysterious.

"Ethan, tell me, tell me. C'mon, I want to know!" Addison couldn't contain her excitement about learning my secret.

"Okay, but you have to swear, Girl Scout's honor and all that stuff, that you won't tell a soul, not anyone."

"I promise, cross my heart and hope to die, stick a needle in my eye. I swear, Ethan. Now tell me." Addison usually didn't whine like this, so I knew she was intrigued.

The sound of wind chimes let me know we were close to Mr. Goodsmith's house, as well as Mrs. Pickens's.

"Well, I found something the other day at Mrs. Pickens's house."

"You did? What is it?" Addie said, continuing her whine.

"Well, it was a strange pair of glasses—goggles, to be exact," I whispered into Addison's ear in my quietest voice so that no one else would be able to hear me but her.

"Really?" As she said it, I knew her curiosity was on high alert.

"Ethan, honey! Oh, pumpkin bunny!" Mrs. Pickens yelled to me from her second-story window, interrupting our conversation as we neared her house.

"Yes, Mrs. Pickens, I'll be right there," I responded as the warmth crept up my face, hoping she wouldn't carry on with her terms of endearment for the entire neighborhood to hear. It was embarrassing enough for Addison to hear.

"So what about these goggles?" Addison said, urging me to go on. "You want some company today, and you can tell me all about them?"

"No, I'm good." I blurted out the words before I even realized they were coming out or how my response must have sounded to Addison.

"Hey, okay, I get the hint. Heard you loud and clear, Ethan. Geez. Later then," Addison said. I could hear the disappointment and hurt in her voice.

"See you in the morning—same time, same channel," I said, hoping to ease a little of what had just happened.

Addison muttered something under her breath that I couldn't make out, and then I heard her footsteps moving farther and farther away, getting quieter and quieter until I could hear them no more. Why was I such a goof when she was around? I knew exactly where she lived, and in my mind, I saw a girl with her head down, carrying her backpack, dejected. I never wanted to hurt Addison, no matter what happened.

"What's up, Lamb Chop?"

"Howdy, Mrs. Pickens. I think I just said the wrong thing to Addison."

"Not to worry. She'll get over it, I'm sure. Now come inside; I have a new snack I want you to try—peanut butter–banana pretzel bites, with chocolate dipping sauce." I heard the sound of the screen door as it opened and knew Mrs. Pickens was standing in the doorway to let me in. This all-too-familiar sound was part of the road map of my life.

"Right behind you," I said. *Note to self: Apologize to Addie in the morning, and tell her everything about the goggles.*

I headed inside, the screen door slamming shut behind me.

CHAPTER 12

ALONE WITH MY GOGGLES

The smells of banana and peanut butter hit me as I entered Mrs. Pickens's house. She had created another new concoction. I was like her recipe guinea pig. It smelled really good in there, but things didn't always taste the way they smelled. Sometimes that was a good thing, and sometimes not so good. The "nots" would wind up in my backpack, discarded in the garbage can when I got back home.

As I made my way to my favorite spot on the couch in the den, a low-humming purr let me know Mrs. Pickens's cat, Katy-do-do, was in her favorite spot on the arm of the couch, dutifully awaiting my arrival. My animal friends were as important to me as some people in my life. My animal friends were like me; they loved with no strings attached.

"Ethan, dear, you don't mind if I run next door, do you? I put a plate of my new recipe on the table where you sit in the den. Mrs. Catalano wants to share her latest recipe, zeppole, with me and give me a quick cooking lesson. I'll bring you back whatever we make."

"Sure, Mrs. P. I'm just going to get started on my homework and then see what I can find out on my laptop about these missing bikes. Have you heard anything?" I said, looking in the direction of her voice.

"Not much, sweetie pie," she said. "But since I don't get out much, working in the library only part-time now, I miss all the goings-on in town. I did hear a blurb on the radio this morning, but I didn't pay it much attention. Well, I'll be back in a jiffy-pop," Mrs. Pickens said with a laugh.

"Later then," I said, getting my laptop out of my backpack and wondering, *What's a jiffy-pop?*

The screen door slammed shut, and through the open window, I heard Mrs. Pickens's footsteps moving down the driveway. She had a heavy footstep, which made me think she was a bit on the chubby side. Now that I was alone, I took the key from around my neck, unlocked the pocket on my backpack that held my goggles, and immediately put them on. Life had become a kaleidoscope of color for me now, and I knew it would take me some time to get used to it all, but I was loving it all the same. My life now was full of light and color, like what I had heard a box of sixty-four Crayolas was like. At times, I felt like I was going to crash like a computer with all this input. Nah!

Opening my laptop, I turned it on and watched as the computer loaded everything. I had JAWS installed on my PC, a program used by the blind, and it had audible technology. It helped me feel as normal as other kids my age, allowing me to access different websites and media, but with the goggles now, I didn't need most of the audio stuff. I used the audio command, and the page quickly loaded for the *Tonawanda Tribune*. I had been a whiz with the computer before, and with the goggles, well, look out!

On the home page of the website was the local news, which the goggles' voice helped me with. As I pointed out certain words with my fingers, the voice read them to me. This still felt kind of weird to me. It was all so different, so new, so *wow*.

I scanned the page, but for the most part, I didn't know what I was looking at, or I wasn't able to read it without the help of the goggles. The goggles seemed to know exactly what I was searching for. Whenever my fingers landed on the page, the voice starting reading out loud to me; Allymom had written this piece.

"Once again police are stumped by the repeated thefts of bicycles in the area." The goggles read down the entire first section, ending with the name of the detective who was handling the case.

> *The Tonawanda Tribune*
> Tuesday: sunny, 68 degrees
> Local News: Tonawanda and Surrounding Cities
> "Missing Bikes Have Police Stumped"
> by Allison Pero
>
> Once again police are stumped by the repeated thefts of bicycles in the area. A total of 15–20 bicycles have been reported missing since early August. The missing bicycles do not seem to share any similar distinguishing factors. The bikes have gone missing from all areas in town, mostly during the late evening hours. There have been no witnesses, and the police have no leads on any of the thefts. The police do ask that if anyone has any details regarding these thefts they call the Theft Hotline at 1-800-Theft-U-2. Contact: Detective James Pardee.

As my finger got to the end of the article, the voice coming from the goggles guided me on what to do. "In order to load another page, move the cursor here." I watched as a symbol moved around the screen and clicked on a line at the bottom of the article. Katy-do-do seemed to like the cursor thing more than I, following it wherever it went on the screen and putting her paw on the screen to try to catch it. I moved it again just for fun, and she moved her head and eyes. I laughed to see her having this much fun. I guess this was how other kids my age used the computer, and now I was going to do the same.

This whole missing-bikes thing actually went further back than the kids at my school even knew about, and my mind sizzled with the excitement of it all. "Fifteen to twenty bikes missing," I said out loud.

"Contact Detective James Pardee, contact number 1-800-345-9876," said the voice, urging me to do what I knew I had to do. I didn't know how I was going to remember all this stuff, how to keep all these things straight in my head.

"Push button on goggles, just above your right eye," the voice continued.

I got up from where I was sitting and went to the mirror in the den. Reaching my hand up, I pushed the button as the voice had told me to.

"This is a voice-activation button. Tell the goggles what you need to find, and it will audio-replay anything that the goggles have seen or heard while you have been wearing them."

"No way," I said out loud. "This is so neat." Just then, I heard the screen door slam and knew Mrs. Pickens was back.

"Hey, Scooby-Doo, where are you?" Mrs. Pickens yelled to me. Mrs. Pickens always yelled when she talked to me. This seemed to be a side effect of my being blind. People always thought if you couldn't see, then you couldn't hear them either. Funny how that worked.

"In here!" I yelled back to her, knowing she would easily find me, since I was always in the same place. My detective work would have to wait a little longer.

"I brought you a goody, right out of the oven, Ethan—zeppole," Mrs. Pickens said as her footsteps got closer. "My oh my, those sure are crazy goggles you've got on."

I sat silently for a moment, stunned, because in addition to being caught wearing the goggles, I was seeing Mrs. Pickens for the first time. She was chubby, but in a nice sort of way. She had a strange smile on her face as I quickly moved to take the goggles off and place them in my lap.

"Oh ... oh ... these old things," I said, hoping I covered my shock at being caught wearing the goggles. "I found these the other day, and I was just goofing around. I'm going to use them for my Halloween costume—Orville Wright, in the flesh."

"I see, Ethan, or do I?" Mrs. Pickens said in a very mysterious-sounding voice, not her usual cheery voice. "I used to have a pair of goggles just like that many years back. Haven't thought about them forever. Mr. Goodsmith and I—well, we used to play with them, but that's a story for another day and time."

"You and Mr. Goodsmith?" I asked.

"Yes, me and Mr. Goodsmith, Ethan. Well, you'd better be on your way. Your mom will be home soon, and you know how she likes to find you safe and sound, like a bug in a rug."

I collected all my things and put the goggles back in my backpack. I grabbed a zeppole off the dish that I had seen when Mrs. P. came into the room.

"A sweet treat for my walking-home feet," I said as I went out the back door of Mrs. P.'s house. *Oh gosh,* I thought, *I'm beginning to sound like Mrs. P.* "See ya mañana."

"De la mañana, it is," I heard Mrs. Pickens say just before the screen door slammed shut.

Twenty, nineteen, eighteen ... the steps to home passed quickly.

CHAPTER 13

WORK TO BE DONE

When I arrived at the back of my house, my fingers reached for the code box, and I entered the code easily on the Braille keypad to the left of the back door. I heard the lock click and opened the door.

The banging of pots and pans and the closing of the oven door let me know Allymom was home early and was already in the kitchen starting on dinner.

"That you, Ethan?" she called out.

"Yep, it sure is," I said. "And I'm starving. Didn't realize I was hungry until I smelled your delicious cooking."

"Yeah, yeah, yeah," Allymom said. I could hear the smile on her face as she responded. Being blind gave me that edge; it let me really hear what and how people said things, I guess much like facial expressions helped people who could see. But that was just a hunch of mine.

"Go wash your hands, Ethan, and dinner will be ready by the time you get back."

"Will do," I said as I made my way to the bathroom. I washed up quickly because I wanted to get back to the important things I needed to get done: eat, get my goggles, and resume solving the bike mystery. I had a mission now, and I felt like there was no stopping me. I was in third gear, driving without brakes on an unknown road, with no road signs or map to guide me, and I couldn't think of anywhere else I would want to be.

Dinner went by quickly, since we were both hungry, and little was said.

"You okay, Ethan?" Allymom questioned. "You're awfully quiet for you. Anything going on that you want to talk about?"

"Nope, it's all good, Allymom." I put a big, super-duper smile on my face to avoid suspicion that anything was up. I felt like a spy playing an undercover role, and I could not be found out.

"Okay, I have some work to do in my office on that bike issue, but the dishes come first," Allymom said. The sound of her chair being pushed along the floor signaled that I could get up too, without fuss. Allymom had an article to write, and I had investigating to do. Big investigating, important investigating, junior crime-solver stuff and all.

I quickly dried the dishes after Allymom washed them and then put them on the kitchen table. I knew where some of the things belonged, but as long as I dried them, Allymom was all right with putting them away. After a few mishaps with broken dishes, I'm sure Allymom thought it was just wiser, not to mention cheaper, if she put them away. Hey, that worked for me!

Done in no time at all, we both made our way upstairs, me to my room and Allymom to hers. I could hear her hitting the keys on her laptop in no time, and she was humming a tune before I could even get my goggles out. For some reason, it was never a song I knew. She had once told me they were all "oldies but goodies." Sometimes I wasn't too sure.

Sitting down at my desk, I reached for my laptop and then realized I had left my backpack downstairs in the kitchen. As I headed toward the stairs, I heard Allymom's voice and realized she was on the phone with Detective Pardee. I stood outside her door, eavesdropping.

"Jim, any new leads on this case? Big Lou is breathing down my neck for answers. The town's starting to buzz with concerns about all this, and you know what that means—only puts more pressure on you and me."

I could hear a male voice responding to her on her phone but couldn't make out what he was saying.

"I see," Allymom said. "Well, keep in touch, and I will too."

I heard her hang up the phone, and her fingers resumed their tapping on the keyboard.

I continued down the stairs and found my backpack where I had left it in the back hall. I unlocked the outside flap with the key from around my neck and took out the case that held the goggles. It was a risk, but I put them on. I reached for the button on the goggles and pushed it to start the replay of all that had happened so far. I needed to get all the details straight in my head.

"Ethan, is that you?" Allymom yelled from her room.

"Yeah," I said quickly. "Just grabbing my backpack." She must have heard the voice, and I realized I had to be more careful.

Back upstairs in the safety of my room, I headed straight for my laptop and stared at the screen for a minute or two, not because I didn't have enough to write but because the realization of all that was changing in my life hit me like a lead brick. *Amazing, truly amazing,* I thought. I didn't even know what half the stuff I was looking at was, but I was learning. I guess it's true what they say: life has a mind of its own, and it can change in a matter of moments. My life was proof of that. It was changing with each minute that ticked away, and I was living it—in living color, no less. I was living my dream, and I couldn't wait to see where it would take me.

CHAPTER 14

CHIME CLUES

My mind started to wander again, and I got up and walked over to the bedroom window. Looking out, I saw what I knew had to be the moon. It looked huge in the sky, a big orb lighting up the night sky.

"The moon formed nearly 4.5 billion years ago. It is Earth's natural satellite and the fifth-largest moon in the solar system. It is round in shape, always showing the same face, and the only celestial body other than Earth on which humans have set foot." The voice was a wealth of knowledge, and I was a quick learner.

The twinkling of lights in the sky could only be the stars Allymom had referred to so often when I was little—"Twinkle, twinkle, little star," she would sing to me. I recited the entire rhyme in my head as I continued to stare at them. The brightness was almost too much for me to see. My eyes blinked several times as they shone so brightly, twinkling on and off. They were like tiny lightbulbs in the sky. When I squinted to see farther down the street, the goggles automatically adjusted to my visual cue. Mr. Goodsmith's house was easily recognizable from where I stood as the open window brought the wind chimes to my ears and a cool breeze to my face.

The goggles once again sensed that I needed to see more detail, and the wind chimes came into focus, with the voice telling me all about them, down to the smallest details. The chimes sounded like a song, and I could hear the hollow tinkling of my favorite one. It was just as Mr. Goodsmith had described it to me: a man holding an umbrella, dancing in the rain, as the metal raindrops chimed along, with the light wind serving as conductor. It was a noise that always sounded happy to me. Mr. Goodsmith said a good chime was all in the planning.

Planning—yes, planning, I thought. That's what I would need to solve this mystery. Scanning the remaining chimes with my goggles, I stopped abruptly, blinking twice to make sure I was seeing what I thought I was seeing. All this vision stuff was so new to me. Before, I could depend only on what I had read and on the mental images I created in my mind without vision. Now all that had changed. With the help of the goggles, I just stopped and stared.

What is that? I wondered. *No, it couldn't be, could it? Does he always use those things in his chimes?*

The voice identified each part for me, but I still couldn't believe what I was seeing. The voice must have got it wrong. It just couldn't be. No way. I blinked twice, and I knew that what I was looking at was exactly what the voice had described. I put my hands on the windowsill, trying to steady not only my body but also my thoughts to keep them from running in all sorts of directions. A supersleuth never jumped to conclusions—well, at least Batman and Superman never did. They always thought things through, and if I was going to be like them, well, I would have to do the same.

"Ethan, it's just about that time," Allymom called from her room down the hall, interrupting my runaway thoughts.

"Okay," I responded. "Going to bed now." For the first time, I felt relieved that I had a curfew. Laughing to myself, I thought, *Well, that's a first.*

As I walked into the hallway leading to the bathroom, I made sure Allymom was nowhere in sight, as I was still wearing the goggles. The coast was clear as I entered the bathroom and quickly shut the door behind me. I brushed my teeth, changed my clothes, went back to my room, and got into bed. I put the goggles away for safekeeping. This was one tired supersleuth, for sure.

I wanted to turn off my brain for a while; there was so much to think about. I felt like a human sponge, trying to absorb everything, and pretty soon something was going to start dripping out. My brain would not shut off, and I kept thinking about what I had seen outside the window down at Mr. Goodsmith's house.

I didn't realize how tired I was till a big yawn overtook me, but a burning question still gnawed at me. Why were all those things a part of Mr. Goodsmith's chimes? Did he always use those things? Was this something new for him? All these questions!

I was exhausted by all that had gone on lately. I had to sleep. My head felt heavy, and I was barely able to stay awake any longer.

Tomorrow's a new day, I thought as I slowly drifted off to sleep.

CHAPTER 15

PUTTING THE GOGGLES TO WORK

The wet slobber from Tucker's tongue licking my face told me it was morning. This dog clearly had some internal clock because he woke me up just about every day, most times even before my alarm clock did. He was on my bed, his front legs straddling my face, with his soft, furry paws touching both of my ears. It felt like I was wearing earmuffs.

"Stop that, Tucker. I think I can wash my own face now," I said, laughing out loud. This was the game we played almost every morning, and I wasn't sure who liked it more, him or me. As I began to pet him, he plopped down right on my stomach, his tail wagging back and forth and slapping my legs, and I felt a sudden urge to get to the bathroom. Tucker's weight on me made my bladder feel like it would burst. Tucker's whimpering plea told me he had to go too.

Pushing him and the blankets off me, I got out of bed, still yawning and wiping the sleep from my eyes. The thoughts of the previous night returned. I felt confused. How could this be? Had I imagined the whole thing? Somewhere deep down inside me, I knew I hadn't. The voice from the goggles had confirmed what I had seen on Mr. Goodsmith's chimes: bicycle parts. Yes, spokes, chains, and gears. I kept wondering if he had always used these parts.

As happy as I was about being able to see with my goggles, a feeling of sadness came over me for a moment, and I shook my head, wanting to stop my thoughts from heading in the wrong direction. Recalling something I had read in one of my Braille textbooks, I said it out loud, hoping to convince myself as I spoke: "Never feel sorry for yourself or others, as things could always be worse." Isn't that the truth!

Slipping my feet into my flip-flops, I made my way to the bathroom, grabbing my goggles along the way. Tucker followed along, his nails *click-clacking* on the wood floors. His continued whimpering alerted me to his own urgent need to go outside.

"Okay, okay," I said. "Let me go, and then it's your turn." With the goggles on, I looked at my buddy a little closer.

"A Lhasa apso," the voice said again. "Guards of the Tibetan castles. Loyal to their masters."

Yeah, that's what I was: his master. He was my loyal sidekick, and that fit right into my plan—a superhero and his faithful companion, Tucker. I pictured Tucker with a little red cape and laughed.

"You'd like that, little buddy, wouldn't you? A little red cape. You could be my own little mighty dog." He would love that. Tucker was a dog you could do anything to, and his tail never stopped wagging. Last Halloween, we had put bat ears on him, and he was my loyal sidekick then too!

Done in the bathroom, I made my way into the hall. There was a small cubbyhole just before the stairs started, and Allymom had placed another audible clock there, but with the goggles on, I could see that it was still early. The soft snore coming from behind Allymom's closed door indicated she was still sleeping, and I was glad to have this time alone.

"Ethan, women don't snore," Allymom had told me once. I laughed to myself as I remembered her words. *Sure, they do*, I thought, and now I had the proof to back it up, since the goggles were recording all the audio I heard.

I made my way down the stairs and into the kitchen, still wearing the goggles, and unlocked the door and opened the screen. Tucker raced past me and into the fenced yard. I sat on the porch in silence, watching Tucker roaming the backyard. It was dark still, and the sounds of the birds awakening and the crickets chirping filled the air. I was at peace sitting there. I sat there for a few moments more, taking it all in.

Tucker nuzzled at my legs, signaling he was done, and I grabbed his leash, which was hanging by the back door next to the keypad, and attached it to his collar. Things like that were so easy for me that I didn't even need the goggles to do them.

As I walked up to the front of the house, Tucker followed along behind me on his leash, sniffing here and there in the grass. I heard the familiar sound of Tony S.'s bicycle before I even saw it. As it passed us, I could see the man clearly, with his wiry, uncombed gray hair and unshaven face.

"Tony S., fifty-eight years old, homeless, five foot eight, thin build. Safety risk: none."

Safety risk? Why had the voice alerted me to this fact? Tony S. was pedaling toward us, again pulling another bike behind him. That still seemed weird—really weird.

"Hey there, Ethan. Those are some snazzy goggles you got there," Tony S. yelled to me, but he didn't miss a beat in his pedaling. "Whatcha doing up so early?"

"Uh ... the dog had to pee," I yelled back, hoping I wouldn't wake up Allymom or any of the neighbors.

"Well, when you gotta go, you gotta go, I always say." He chuckled and then sped on down the street, the other bike trailing behind him.

My supersleuth radar was on full blast. Mr. Goodsmith? Tony S.? Was one of them the bike thief? "Voice recorder," I said, "make a note under the heading 'Suspect List': One, Mr. Goodsmith. Two, Tony S."

How could two suspects be so different?

CHAPTER 16

DETECTIVE STUFF

Making my way down the driveway and onto the sidewalk, I caught myself counting steps and realized good habits are hard to break. As I approached Mr. Goodsmith's house, everything I had seen the night before came into view and was crystal clear. There it all was, plain as day, with all his wind chimes swaying in the breeze.

"Bicycle parts," the voice said. It then reviewed all that it had identified the previous night. "Seat, crossbar, stem, brake cable, brake lever, down tube, hub, rim, tire valve, pedal, crank arm, chain ring ..."

"Bicycle parts," I whispered, nodding, realizing that what I'd thought I'd seen at night was exactly what I was seeing now. "How could this be? What does this all mean?" I said quietly.

Tucker looked at me like he thought I really expected him to answer me. He sat down next to me on the sidewalk, his tail wagging as fast as my thoughts were moving.

I need to remain calm, I reminded myself. Breathing in and out slowly, I realized I needed to rein in my thoughts before they got too far ahead of me. I tried coming up with a logical explanation for what I saw but couldn't. There seemed to be only one explanation, and I didn't like where it was leading me.

Mr. Goodsmith had gotten his parts for his wind chimes from all different places, and in my gut, I knew something was up.

Just at that moment, the sun began to rise in the sky, and the glare shone on the wind chimes, making me look away for a moment. *Wow, that's bright!* I was so preoccupied that I almost stepped on Tucker but instead tripped and sat down hard on the wet grass. "Sorry, little buddy," I said.

Tucker glanced in my direction for a second and then continued sniffing the grass, uninterested in the unfolding events.

Sitting cross-legged on Mr. Goodsmith's lawn, I leaned back on the big maple tree behind me, glad for its mighty support. The rough-edged bark dug into my back, but I sat there for a while, just looking at all the chimes, my eyes scanning back and forth, amazed by what I was looking at and confused about what it all meant.

My preset alarm on my watch signaled to me that I needed to get back home and get ready for school. I stood up and scanned the chimes once more before heading home.

"Bicycle parts," the goggles said again.

Walking on the sidewalk away from Mr. Goodsmith's house, I felt like I was being watched, and the hairs on the back of my neck stood up straight. I looked back over my shoulder in the direction of his house and saw the shadowy outline of a man in the front window as the curtain slowly closed. The shadow remained behind the pale, sheer curtain, unflinching.

The voice said in a low monotone, "Mr. Goodsmith, eighty years old, neighbor, metalworker, wind chime creator, and friend. Safety risk: none found at this time."

"Why was he watching me?" I said aloud to myself. "Get a grip on yourself, Ethan. There's gotta be a good explanation for all this." I shook my head back and forth, trying to shake the feeling of paranoia that was rising inside me. It didn't help, and the feeling hung around me, swirling like a sandstorm. I quickened my steps till I reached home. I had hoped to slip back in the back door, unnoticed. But as I got closer, I saw Allymom through the window.

"Allymom," the voice said. "Aunt-mom to Ethan. Five feet seven inches tall, thin build, brown hair, brown eyes. Newspaper reporter at the *Tonawanda Tribune.*"

"Oh, shush," I said to the voice. Looking at Allymom, I realized how lucky I was to have this special person who cared for me when my real mom died. She had stepped in to take on the job and had transformed her life in so many ways, I was sure. It made me wonder if she resembled my real mom.

"And just where have you been, young man, and what are those unusual glasses you're wearing?" Allymom's voice was stern and firm as I watched her as she stood in the doorway of our house. I didn't hear this tone too often, but when I did, I knew it could mean trouble.

"Uh, well, Tucker wanted to go for a longer walk this morning, and since I woke up early, I thought it would be okay. And these old things, they're nothing. I found them the other day at Mrs. Pickens's house, and she said that I could keep them. Neat, huh?"

"Neat, they are, Ethan. The bike thefts are continuing, and I wouldn't want you to come across anyone in the early hours of the day in the act of trying to steal them. You need to be careful out there. Times sure are changing. Hard to believe, but they are." Allymom said this with a bit of melancholy in her voice, a wistfulness.

I hoped she wasn't going to start reminiscing about yesteryear, not that I didn't want to hear what it used to be like in this town, but it was just that I had so much thinking to do before school, and sometimes she would go on and on, and there would be no stopping her.

"All right," I said, quickly moving past her and hoping this would cut the lecture short. It worked, and I took the goggles off as I made my way upstairs. I needed to be more careful with these things.

"Breakfast in five, Ethan, and no dawdling." Allymom started to busy herself in the kitchen, finishing up breakfast.

Tucker was close behind me, as I could hear each of his steps as he followed along. Grabbing my backpack and all the things I would need for school, I made my way back downstairs, grabbed my breakfast to eat on the way, and headed out the door, just as I heard Addison coming up the driveway.

"Sheesh, someone is sure eager to get to school today. So tell me about those glasses you found, Ethan. I can't wait to hear the whole story," Addison said to me just as we made our way down the driveway and onto the sidewalk that would take us the short distance to school.

I reached into my backpack and put the goggles on. "That sure is a pretty pink sweater you're wearing today, Addison," I said.

"Thanks, Ethan. Wait, what? I mean ... I mean," Addison said, stuttering and staring at me. "What do you mean, 'That's a nice pink sweater you have on'? How ... I mean, when ... I mean, how ... I mean, when ..." Addie grabbed me by the shoulders and pulled me close to her so that our noses were almost touching.

"I told you I had a secret for you, Addison." I laughed, but her face was priceless. "Well, you know I told you I found a pair of goggles at Mrs. Pickens's house, right? Well, I didn't tell you how I found them or what they can do." I went on to tell Addison the whole story, from start to finish. Her eyes were wide, and her mouth hung open the whole time. "You can close your mouth now, Addison," I said when I was done.

"Oh my gosh, Ethan. This is super exciting. Let me see them; let me see them!" she said excitedly.

I took the goggles off, but not before seeing her eyes become big black orbs.

"Ethan, these are the coolest things ever. Just imagine what this means for you!" Addison sounded as excited as I had been when I found the goggles. It was fun to watch and hear her reaction.

"See?" I said. "Now I'm just like you—well, almost like you."

"Here, Ethan, put them back on," Addison said. "I can't believe this. What does it all mean?"

I went on to explain everything I had seen and learned about since finding the goggles. Addie stood there, speechless, with her mouth and eyes both open wide. "Yep," I said, "Ethan Pero is able to see! In living color, no doubt. These are so cool, Addison. The goggles are teaching me new things all the time about this new life with vision. It's so darn cool. And you know what else?"

"Ethan, isn't that enough?" She giggled happily.

I got closer to Addison and whispered into her ear, "Nope, it isn't enough. I'm going to try to solve this bike mystery—with your help too, if you want."

"I'm in," Addison said. She sounded as excited as I did.

I took off the goggles as we approached the school grounds because I didn't want to have to answer questions from anybody else right now.

"Gosh, Ethan, what can happen next? What next?" she said as we went through the school doors just as the bell rang.

CHAPTER 17

THE LONG WEEKEND

School went by without a hitch, and I was glad that it was Friday, not to mention a long weekend, with a teacher planning day on Monday. That meant no school for the next couple of days— plenty of time to work on or even solve this mystery. Friday also meant that I would be going directly home because Mrs. Pickens had her knitting club that night.

The first thing I needed to do was call that detective for more information. I was hoping Allymom's name would help me navigate some of the roadblocks I might encounter. Being a reporter, she spoke with the police all the time, and when I thought about it, I remembered that I had met this detective last year at one of the town's fairs. Everything seemed to be falling into place for me to get things done.

Picking up the phone as soon as I walked in the house, I dialed the 1-800 number with the help of my goggles and the voice.

"Tonawanda Police Department, nonemergency line," a woman said. "This line is recorded. May I help you?"

"Hello, my name is Ethan Pero. I would like to speak with Detective Pardee."

"I'll transfer you. Please hold."

I waited on hold for what seemed like forever, humming along with the patriotic song being played on the line.

"Tonawanda PD, Detective Pardee. How can I help you?"

"Hi, hello, Detective Pardee," I said, stammering slightly before I regained my composure. "Hi, I'm Ethan Pero. Allison Pero is my mom, and I wanted to ask you some questions about the missing-bike problem in the area. I'm ... I'm doing a report on theft for one of my classes, and I think this is just the thing that will help me get an A."

"Well, Son, there's really not too much to tell right now. We have a multitude of missing bikes and no leads or trails, except that they all seem to go missing late at night and in the early morning hours, and the real odd thing about all this is that a brand-new bike shows up the next day to replace the one taken. No witnesses, no nothing. I tell you, the parents have mixed feelings about all this, and ... and no doubt, some bike shop somewhere is busier than ever." The detective chuckled at this last remark.

"It does seem odd, don't you think, that you have no clues for any of these missing bikes?" I asked curiously, hoping he would divulge more of the case to me because I knew there had to be more than he was letting on.

"It's a mystery, all right—a dang-gone mystery, I tell ya."

I realized that the detective was not going to give in. "Okay. Well, thank you for your time, sir. Would it be all right if I kept in touch with you on this?" I crossed my fingers, hoping he would say yes.

"Sure, Son. You call me anytime you like, and if you hear anything at school, you let me know too." I then heard the line go dead; the detective had hung up.

I stared at the phone, realizing I was really no further ahead than before the call, with no further leads or information. I dialed up a few of the local bike shops, but none had experienced any spurt in sales, especially from any one person. I had questions, and I needed answers, and I needed them yesterday. I felt up for this mission—a mission that surely had clues that were being missed and that I could locate. It was just a feeling, but I didn't think the police were going to share anything with me.

Tucker started his whimpering chant, so I grabbed his leash and my goggles and headed out the door.

It was late in the afternoon, and the sun was casting just a small amount of a pinkish-yellow hue on what I knew had to be the horizon. The voice confirmed my thoughts—"Horizon, the apparent line that separates the earth from the sky"—while showing me an identical picture in the corner of the right eye of the goggles.

The leaves in the trees were rustling in the gently blowing wind, and the leaves on the ground looked like they were dancing across the grass. The voice told me these were maple trees, very common in this part of the Northeast.

I headed once more in the direction of Mr. Goodsmith's house, and my steps were in rhythm with his wind chimes, which grew louder with each step as I moved closer and closer to his house.

"Now that's quite a pair of spectacles you have there, Son." I stopped abruptly, staring at Mr. Goodsmith as he stood on his front porch and trying to think of something to say. "I ... I ... I suppose they are. I'm ... I'm going to use them for my Halloween costume. I'm going as one of the Wright Brothers, and these are my flight goggles." I tried to sound as convincing as I could, but with the goggles on, I could see that Mr. Goodsmith was not convinced. His stare deepened, and it felt like he could see that I was not telling him the truth. It's like people are born with these little lie detectors built inside them, that become active when they are adults.

Mr. Goodsmith just stood there, waiting for me to go on. This was the second time I had actually seen him, and he was tall, really tall. The goggles identified all the parts of his face to me, down to the wrinkles and creases that lined his wise-looking face. Allymom told me that such lines showed that people had lived long and interesting lives. They added character, she said. His eyes looked friendly, and he had a slight smile on his face, almost like he was testing me. But there was nothing to be afraid of when it came to Mr. Goodsmith; he was a good guy in my eyes.

"Yep, Halloween, that's just what these goggles are for." I felt the need to say it again with as much conviction as I could so that maybe I would believe it was true too.

The glare of the sun hit my goggles again just as I finished talking, and it blinded me for a second. It didn't feel all that strange, for a blind world was the norm to me. The wind chimes came into focus just as a cloud moved over the sun. But these were all different ones than I had seen the night before. Where were all the bicycle chimes?

Staring at them, I suddenly realized that Mr. Goodsmith had been talking, and I had missed everything he'd said. I nodded back, hoping he hadn't caught on to the fact that I hadn't been listening.

A tug on Tucker's leash reminded me that Tucker was not done with his walk. As he started to pull me away, I was glad to have an excuse to leave. "Well, gotta go, Mr. Goodsmith. Allymom will be calling the house soon to make sure I got home all right. You know how it is—she'll have the whole town searching for me if I'm not home when she calls," I said with a smile and a laugh.

"I guess you're right, young man." Mr. Goodsmith laughed too.

"See ya around," I yelled to him as I waved and walked away.

I heard Mr. Goodsmith talking to himself as I left, something about work to be done later that night in the garage. Even with the goggles, my ears were still my best asset; they were razor-sharp listening machines.

"Voice," I whispered, "make note to self: stakeout tonight." As my curiosity went into high alert, I wanted to make sure I didn't forget a thing, and the goggles made that easier.

"Yes, sir," responded the voice. "Noted and logged."

Mr. Goodsmith was definitely a suspect, along with Tony S. They were both on my watch list, and I needed to follow their every move—as best as I could anyway. My crime-solver instincts told me something was just not right. Mr. Goodsmith couldn't have sold all those bike chimes in one day. Sometimes he told me he hadn't made a sale in weeks. So where had all those wind chimes gone?

The question played over and over in my head as I made my way back home. *Where did they all go?*

CHAPTER 18

NIGHT OF ESPIONAGE

Walking home, I was struck by how my world was changing and how the choices I was making would have a major impact on my life. I was keeping my fingers crossed that solving this mystery would help me somehow fit in better with other kids.

I might have been only eleven, but I wanted to finally feel like the puzzle piece that fit perfectly into the whole scheme of things, and not the piece that you tried to squeeze into the puzzle and bent because it didn't quite fit. Have you ever felt that way? I doubt I'm the only one. I didn't want to be the most popular kid in school; I just wanted to feel that I fit in a bit better than I did. I didn't want to be the quarterback, but I was definitely tired of being the one always sitting on the bench, if you know what I mean. I was close, but this would bring me even closer.

I reached the back door of my house quickly, and I was glad I would be alone for a bit. Allymom was still at the newspaper office with deadlines to meet for the weekend edition. I had things to plan and things to do, like update my file on the computer and plan the latest espionage.

First things first though, I thought as I reached for my phone and used the voice activation for Addison's number. Old habits were still hard to break.

"Addison, hey, it's me, Ethan."

"Ethan, you say that every time, and each time I tell you I have caller ID," she said.

"I know, I know. Hey, are you up for some supersleuthing tonight with me?"

"Sure. What do you have in mind?"

"I went by Mr. Goodsmith's house, and everything was different, Addison. All the chimes I saw last night were gone. Vanished. M-I-A! Mr. Goodsmith was talking to himself, and I heard him say he had work to do tonight. Addison, a stakeout is needed tonight! We have espionage work to get done."

"What do you think he's up to?"

"I'm not sure, but I'm going to find out, one way or another. Are you in?"

"I'm in, I'm in," Addison said excitedly. "What's the plan?"

"Well, Allymom doesn't get home until around nine or so— you know, it being Friday and all. But then Mrs. Pickens stops by around six thirty to bring me dinner and then sometimes calls me close to eight thirty to make sure I'm okay. So we can't leave before she brings me dinner, and I have to be back here before Allymom gets home. So here's the plan: come pick me up around six forty-five. I'll have my goggles with me, and you bring a flashlight; we may need it. Oh yeah, and wear dark clothes. We don't want to risk being seen."

"Ethan, slow down. I know you can't believe all this is happening, but take a breath every now and then, okay?" Addison said in a slow and steady mom-like voice.

"I know, I know, but it's just so exciting and all. It's what I've always wanted, like a dream come true. We have a mission that needs to get accomplished tonight. Let's concentrate on that for now. We must maintain focus," I said with a laugh, using my Principal Robertson voice for added effect. Darth Vader had nothing on me.

"Oh, Ethan, you're so dramatic. I'll see you at six forty-five."

"Roger that." And with that, I hung up the phone and walked back over to my bedroom window.

I played it over and over in my head, what I had seen the night before at Mr. Goodsmith's house and what I had seen that day. Still wearing the goggles, I zoomed in on Mr. Goodsmith's porch, and there he stood, staring right in my direction while putting up another wind chime. I ducked quickly below the window frame but still got a glimpse of the chime in his hands. The long tubes of metal hanging off the chime in a U shape, with small keys dangling from the tubes' ends, were easily recognizable.

"Bicycle parts. He's testing my sleuthing skills, but why?"

"Bicycle parts," the voice repeated, apparently thinking I had made a request. A picture of a bike showed up in my goggles, identifying all the parts of a bike to me: saddle seat, seat clamp, rim, hub, brake, fork, skewer, pedal, and on and on. I recognized some of these from the chimes I had seen the night before, and here they were again.

"Voice, that wasn't a request. That was a statement of fact."

"My apologies, sir," the voice responded quickly.

I wanted to look out the window again. I needed to see just what Mr. Goodsmith was up to. I crouched on my knees and inched my head up the wall till I could just peek out the window. With my eyes barely above the windowsill, I saw him still standing there. Luckily, he was looking in the other direction now.

"What is he up to?" I said out loud as I moved to my desk, ready to update my file on my computer. Just then, the phone rang.

"Hi there, young man. How was your day?" said Allymom when I answered.

"Doesn't get any better than this. And yours?"

"Well, I finished my article and then got a very interesting call from Detective Pardee."

My stomach sank a bit.

"He told me about your conversation, and I was surprised you hadn't mentioned anything to me."

"Well, you know me and a good mystery. I wanted to see if he could add any more details about the missing bikes that I didn't already know. By the way, Addison is coming over tonight, and we might go to the park or just the playground. Would that be okay?"

"Okay, but be in the house before I get home and no later." Allymom was lenient in some ways and strict in others. She always said she was raising me like her mom had raised her. I hadn't figured out yet if that was going to be a good thing or bad thing for me, but for now, it worked. Tonawanda was still a safe area, she said, so kids roamed easily through the neighborhoods. Parents looked out for everyone here, even other people's kids.

"Bye, Allymom," I said quickly, eager to get off the phone and get prepared for tonight.

The sound of the doorbell interrupted my thoughts again.

"Somewhere over the rainbow," sang Mrs. Pickens, her voice coming through the open window as the smell of her famous chicken potpie alerted my nose to my dinner's arrival. The potpie definitely was the winner in that contest of the senses.

I knew that she would leave it on the back porch, as always, so I made my way down the stairs. Mrs. Pickens had her knitting club on Fridays, promptly at 6:45 p.m., so it was a drop-and-run, as usual.

Still wearing the goggles—life was a tad bit easier with them—I made my way to the back door to get my dinner. The warming bag containing dinner was just where it always was, to

79

the left of the back door. As I reached down to pick it up, the phone rang again.

Geez, can't I catch a break here? I thought as I reached for the phone on the wall. "Hi, Addison," I said before she could even speak. "See, I have caller ID too."

"Okay, goggle-man," she said with a laugh. "Count to twenty, and I'll be there in a skip and a jump."

CHAPTER 19

NIGHT SLEUTHING

Eighteen, nineteen, twenty. I counted the last few seconds in my head, and the doorbell rang just as I finished the count.

"Come on in, Addison," I said with a mouth full of food. Tucker came bouncing into the room for his fair share, his tail in motion, as always. Tucker always knew when I was eating potpie or a pizza from Bocce's, the best spot in Buffalo. Allymom was pretty strict about feeding Tucker table food, but she gave in when it came to these two things, potpie and pizza crust, and I was glad because his whimpering was relentless until you gave in.

"Hey, Ethan. You all ready to go?"

"Yep, just have to grab my backpack, and I'll be ready to hit the pavement." I ran up the stairs to grab my backpack and shut down my computer. I couldn't let anyone catch a glimpse of anything yet, especially Allymom. I knew I would have to tell her when the time was right, but just not now.

"Ready?" Addison said as I came back into the kitchen.

"Ready, Freddie," I said.

"You'd better watch out, Ethan. Mrs. Pickens is rubbing off on you."

We both laughed as we walked out the back door. I heard the sound of the automatic door lock clicking into place behind us.

81

"You have the flashlight?" I asked, looking directly at Addison. Still not used to having sight, I found myself staring at her and had to force myself to look away.

"Yes. I hope there won't be anything else we need, but I think between your goggles and the flashlight, we're good to go. And stop looking at me like that, Ethan," she said with a smirk on her face, crossing her eyes.

"It's hard not to," I said, smiling. My heart was flip-flopping in my chest as I watched her.

"I know it must be weird, seeing me and all, Ethan," Addie said, blushing, as she gave me a light shove. "But stop it already. Sheesh."

We both laughed. For me, it was to hide my nervousness; for Addison, I wasn't really sure.

"We need some good investigating tonight, Ethan. We're supersleuths, and that's all we need to concentrate on right now."

We continued to make our way down the driveway to Mr. Goodsmith's house. The streets were unusually quiet, especially since it was pretty early, and there was no school the next day. But this worked in our favor; fewer people seeing us was a good thing.

Our luck was holding out for now. The streetlights came on just like clockwork, although it was still light enough outside to see. Later on, they would help to create the shadows we would need to hide in. It was like a sign everything would be all right. It was like a supersleuth's paradise.

"Whatcha doing, P-Pero?" Mikey's voice came from behind the bushes that divided our house from our neighbors' property. Addison and I both turned in the direction of his voice.

"Oh no, Ethan," Addison whined. "He's going to spoil everything."

"Well, not if we don't let him," I whispered in her ear as an idea took form in my head. "Why don't we just include him—make him a part of our supersleuthing team? It's better for him to be on our side than against us, don't you think? But he'll have to swear to secrecy first."

"No way, Ethan. Do you think you can ever trust him again?"

Lost in thought, I didn't respond right away.

"Earth to Ethan. I'm talking to you!" Addison gave me a shove, jarring me out of my thoughts.

"I really think it's what we both need to make us friends again. It's a leap of faith, I know, but I'm willing to take the chance. Like Mr. Goodsmith always tells me, 'Everyone deserves a second chance, but smart people stop at a third one.' This is me giving Mikey a second chance, okay?"

Just then, Mikey leaped onto the sidewalk from his hiding place in the bushes. "Grrr!" Mikey roared, as if he were the Kraken from *Clash of the Titans*.

Addison screamed and jumped back, just about knocking me over. It took all my strength not to lose my balance, but I stood my ground. I needed to show Mikey who was in charge. I couldn't let him see me rattled, not now.

"Wow, Mikey, that was some entrance you made ... you really scared us both." I was hoping that if I complimented Mikey on his latest prank, he'd be more open to my offer.

"How'd you know it was me, P-Pero?" Mikey said.

"Just a lucky guess." I breathed in deeply as I spoke, turning my head to look at Addison.

She held her hand in front of her mouth, trying to conceal her laugh, but her nose, all wrinkled up, said everything. I knew Mikey's scent had reached her too.

"Hey, Mikey, I have a proposition for you," I said, resting my hands on my hips as we stood face-to-face.

"A p-prop-a-what?" Mikey said.

"Proposition, an offer," I explained.

"Okay, tell me about your p-prop-a-dition ... I mean, your o-offer," Mikey said, stumbling over his words. We all had our little differences, and Mikey's stutter was his, but that didn't matter to me.

"Well, if I tell you, you have to swear to secrecy, on your honor and all that stuff. You have to swear that you will not tell a single soul. The three of us will be in this together. We will be honor-bound to a code of secrecy, and if you don't stick to the code of secrecy, you will have to lose something of real importance to you, of my choosing."

Knowing what I was going to take into my possession, into custody, added to the thrill of it all. It would ensure Mikey's loyalty to our group. Mikey's grandfather was a hero from World War II. He had left Mikey a rare coin that he had carried around with him all through his war service and during the attack on Pearl Harbor. His grandfather was one of five men who had survived that day. Mikey carried the coin with him wherever he went, attached to a chain that he wore around his neck. I couldn't remember a time when he wasn't wearing it.

"Okay, tell me what the secret is and what I have to do to join," Mikey said, jumping up and down.

"Okay, okay. Calm down, 'cause you're not going to like it. If you don't abide by the code, you will have to give me your grandfather's coin, the one that you wear around your neck, and then you have to swear that you will keep our secret, on your honor, all that stuff. You up for the challenge, Mikey?"

"I s-swear. I s-swear," Mikey said as he slowly took the chain from around his neck and handed it to me.

"Mikey, raise your right hand, and repeat after me. I, Mikey McGurren, do solemnly swear to the code of secrecy and will relinquish my grandfather's coin if I break my oath, in accordance with the Supersleuth's Pledge of Allegiance."

Mikey repeated the words back to me in the most serious voice I had ever heard from him, without one stutter, as I held the chain in front of him, the coin swinging in the light breeze as if to hypnotize him. I then went on to tell him the whole story about the goggles and my 3-D vision. He stood there with wide eyes and an open mouth, and I knew I had him as I let go of the chain and he caught it midair before it hit the ground.

"N-no way," Mikey said. "How is that even p-possible?"

"It's possible, all right, Mikey," Addison chimed in.

"This is way c-cool, you guys, and now I'm g-gonna be a part of all this." Mikey started bunny-hopping again, up and down the sidewalk. He was hooked like a fish on a line.

"All hands in," I said as I put my hand out in front of me. Addie placed hers on top of mine, and Mikey followed last. *A hand sandwich of solidarity*, I thought.

"We are the Supersleuth Gang," I said. "Our commitment to one another must rise above any other. We will be strong as one. All three here promise to keep our secret safe, and those here pledge loyalty to the gang. All those standing here today say, 'Yeah!'"

"Yeah!" Addie squealed.

"Y-yeah!" Mikey excitedly answered.

And at that moment, our fate was sealed as the Supersleuth Gang.

CHAPTER 20

THE THREE OF US

As all three of us made our way down the street, walking side by side, a team of supersleuths on a mission, we passed Mrs. Pickens's house. I could see her in her front window moving furniture around, but I knew that I wouldn't have to be as careful the next time I was over there, now that I had the goggles. I reached up and lightly touched the healing bruise, which was still a little sore. Luckily enough, it had gone unnoticed, but then again, I was always covered in bumps and bruises, not out of place for this little blind kid from Tonawanda.

Just as we were approaching Mr. Goodsmith's house, Tony S. zoomed by on his bike, again with another bike trailing behind him, this time attached by a short metal chain.

"W-where do you think he's g-going, E-Ethan, with that other b-bike?" Mikey asked. "That's w-weird, don't ya think?"

"He's been doing that a lot lately, Mikey, and it's making me think something's just not right. Maybe after we check out Mr. Goodsmith's house, we can go by where Tony S. stays every night and see what he's up to—that is, if we have time."

"G-good idea, E-Ethan." Mikey sounded like the Mikey I remembered, and I smiled, realizing I had made a good decision in including him in our group. I guessed Mr. Goodsmith was right.

The sound of a door slamming shut brought our attention back to our mission. We saw Mr. Goodsmith coming out of his house and heading toward the backyard. A bike was leaning up against the gate that separated the front yard from the back, and we slowly crept along the shadows, in single file, with me as the lead and Mikey trailing behind.

"A b-bike, Ethan. Will ya look at th-that?"

"Shh, Mikey," Addison whispered.

"B-but what's he doing with that b-bike?"

"Mikey, please, lower your voice," Addison said, sounding like one of the teachers at school.

"O-k-kay."

We watched Mr. Goodsmith as he guided the bike toward his work shed behind the house. We hid behind his parked car in the driveway, with our heads just peering over the trunk of the car.

"Camera ready," said the voice.

"Sh-sheesh, who was th-that?" Mikey asked.

I explained quickly to Mikey about the voice and everything it had helped me with. Having a camera in the goggles would be a lifesaver.

"These things are unbelievable, aren't they, Addison?" I said, looking directly at Addison.

She shrugged her shoulders.

"Point goggles in direction of what you want a picture of. Blink once for quick frame, and blink fast for multiple frames." The voice went on to instruct me all about the camera, video, and print capabilities of the goggles.

I blinked a couple of times in quick succession, with some added instruction coming from the voice.

"Mr. Goodsmith keeps a lot of his chimes that he is working on in that shed, you know," I said. "He's told me a lot about it. Once he gets an idea for a new chime, he keeps all the parts in there until he starts creating it."

The creaking of the shed door opening and closing gave us the signal to move a bit closer, and we inched our way up the driveway, making sure to stay in the shadows of the house. We needed a closer look to get more clues. Just below the shed's window, we found a small bucket that would be perfect to help us get a glimpse into the shed. Stepping onto the overturned bucket, I was able to see Mr. Goodsmith inside, his back to us. I watched as he started to take the bike apart, piece by piece. I watched until the bike was just a pile of metal and rubber sitting in the center of the shed.

"I w-wanna see," Mikey said.

"Shh! Mikey, you have to be quiet, or you're gonna ruin everything. Tell him, Ethan," Addison said.

"Mikey, you have to use your quiet voice—you know, like they tell us in school. This is super important," I said.

Mikey stepped up with one foot on the bucket so that we both could look at the same time. "W-wow, he took that bike apart in no t-time," Mikey said in his best whisper.

I snapped another picture, and the flash in the goggles went off this time, reflecting in the window. "Uh-oh," I said just as Mr. Goodsmith turned around to see where the flash had come from.

Mikey and I both lost our footing and tumbled off the bucket into the soft grass, knocking Addison over as we fell. I moved quickly to help them both get to their feet, but before we could get far, the creaking of the shed door opening made us all stop in our tracks.

"Who's out there?" Mr. Goodsmith questioned. "Don't make me call the police again now."

Mr. Goodsmith had told me that someone or something was breaking into his shed, but he couldn't figure out who or what it was. Nothing was ever taken, he said; he just found things out of place and knocked over onto the shed's floor.

We stood huddled close together in the shadows behind the shed, hoping we wouldn't be discovered, Mikey rubbing his elbow. Looking at Addison and Mikey, I realized we looked like a bunch of balloons ready to burst as we held our breath, not daring to make a sound. I couldn't tell who was shaking the most—me, Addison, or Mikey—as Mr. Goodsmith's footsteps grew closer and closer.

"Who's out there, I say," Mr. Goodsmith shouted, but this time I could see a smirk on his face, almost as if he knew who the mice were and he was the smart, all-knowing, feral cat.

Finally, Mr. Goodsmith turned around and went back into the shed, shaking his head, and we all let out a simultaneous, slow breath of relief.

"Th-that was c-close," Mikey whispered.

"It sure was," I responded. "I guess we have some things to learn about sleuthing and spying."

We returned quietly to the window and saw Mr. Goodsmith examining each part and putting the parts into different piles on his workbench.

"I think we've seen enough for now," I said to my fellow sleuths.

As we headed back down the driveway, we heard the shed door open and close, and we quickly ducked down behind Mr. Goodsmith's car, once again avoiding detection.

"Okay, he's back in the house, Ethan," Addison said a minute later.

"That was close ... again," I said.

"S-sure was," Mikey said. "I guess we g-got some learning to do, like you said, huh, E-Ethan?"

"Ya got that right, Mikey."

Looking back over my shoulder as we all continued to move farther and farther away from the house, I once again saw a shadow of a person behind the curtains in the front window of Mr. Goodsmith's house. That all-too-familiar shiver started its trail down my back, as I knew we were being watched. I chose to keep silent for now.

Music was playing in the distance, and I remembered the concert that was scheduled for that day in the park up the street. "Hey, you want to head over to the park?" I said to Addison and Mikey. "That concert must still be going on. The park is close to where Tony S. stays, just under the bridge, so we might get to see what he's doing from a distance."

"Sure, Ethan," Addison answered, "but remember, your mom wants you back in the house before she gets home."

"We still have time, Addison. Don't be such a worrywart."

The band was still playing when we reached the edge of the park, and we stood together listening to its rendition of a One Republic song. Addison, always thinking ahead, had some snacks with her, so we munched on popcorn and peanuts while we listened.

At the same time the band finished the song, Tony S. zoomed by again with another bike, and this time, we followed him. He seemed to be going in the direction of where he stayed each night.

Addison was at my side, and as her arm brushed mine, I turned to look at her. Was it an accident? She turned to look at me at that same moment, shoving me off the sidewalk and making me lose my balance and fall into the wet grass.

"Knock it off," she said as she offered her hand to help me back up. "You can be so annoying at times, Ethan, but I love ya anyway."

"Ya love me, Addison?" I said, making the funniest face I could think to make.

"You know what I mean," she said, stammering. "Let's keep focused, you two."

There was something I really liked about Addison, and I hoped the feelings were mutual. It felt like we were more than friends, and I was beginning to think she thought so too. Time would tell, I guess.

"C-c'mon, you two. Enough of the l-lovey-d-dovey s-stuff. We have w-work to do," Mikey said.

I realized that when Mikey made more sense than I did, I better get my act together. We finally reached Tony S.'s "home" spot, and what we saw left us all speechless, with our mouths hanging open.

CHAPTER 21

SUSPECT: TONY S.

"I can't believe what I'm seeing," I said. When I turned toward Mikey and Addie, the stunned looks on their faces confirmed that they were as shocked as I was. Bikes and bike parts were lying all around under the bridge. Tony S. was standing in the middle of it all.

"Pete, we got quite a handful of new material today. Ain't that great?" Tony S. said.

"Yeah, yeah, we did good today." Pete was a newfound friend of Tony S.'s. We didn't know much about him. Addison's mom, who worked down at the homeless shelter, said he just showed up one day, new to the area. He didn't tell her much about who he was or where he'd come from. He had only stayed in the shelter a couple of nights.

As the three of us stared in silence over the concrete embankment, Addie and Mikey looked like they had just lost their best friend, and I suspected I looked the same.

"Ethan, I can't believe this. Not Tony S.," Addison whispered.

"Looks like we may have just found another suspect in this bike-theft ring, after all. You think Mr. Goodsmith and Tony S. are in on this together? Seems like an unlikely pair, don't you think?" I said, looking at both of them for an answer.

"F-for s-sure."

"There's got to be an explanation for this, Ethan," Addison said hopefully.

"I can't think of one just yet, but I think we need to make sure we're not jumping to any conclusions. Mr. Goodsmith always told me that what something looks like and what something is can be two totally different things, and the smart thing to do is stand back and think things through. I just didn't think it would be this hard."

Tony S. and Pete began to take some of the bikes apart, and some they didn't, leaving one pile of wheels, handlebars, pedals, and such and another area with bikes whole and ready to ride.

What had we stumbled upon if these were not the stolen bicycles? What else could it be? So many questions were floating around in my head. Two of my favorite people, Mr. Goodsmith and Tony S., might be involved in something that was not good.

"Ethan, you all right?" Addison asked. "You don't look so good."

"Yeah, I guess so. It's just that I feel kind of betrayed, you know? I'm just hoping we're wrong about all this and that there's something else going on here."

"It's a m-mystery, all right, a real who-d-dunit, E-Ethan."

"You got that right, but let's stay focused. Let's go back to my house, and we can try to sort this all out and make a plan."

"It's getting late, Ethan. I think we should just sleep on it and start again tomorrow. With no school, we'll have the whole day to start trying to figure this all out, and maybe we'll be better able to think things through after a good night's sleep."

"G-good, idea, Addie," Mikey said. "Actually, that's a g-great idea."

I took off the goggles as we approached my house, and Addison and Mikey walked me to my back door.

"See ya tomorrow," said Addie.

"Yeah, s-s-see you tomorrow, E-Ethan."

Allymom was still up when I came in. "Guess I beat you home; I got all my work done sooner than I thought. How was your day, big boy? I bet you're happy to be off school for a few days."

"You could say that," I said as I walked into the house. The smell of a Bocce pizza hit my nose as I entered. "You don't mind if I go right up to my room, do you?"

"You must be tired, Ethan, if you're passing on a slice of pizza. You okay?" Allymom had that concerned-mom tone to her voice.

"Sure, I am. Just tired, that's all. Just like you, I've had a long day." As I walked up the stairs, I could tell Allymom was following me with her eyes. I just knew it.

Tomorrow was a new day, and I wanted to be bright-eyed and bushy-tailed, as Mrs. Pickens would say. Too tired even to change my clothes, I got into bed and closed my eyes, hoping to shut off my brain for a while, at least until the next morning.

CHAPTER 22

GI MIKEY

Tap ... tap ... tap.

"What is that?" I said out loud, rubbing the sleep from my eyes. I reached for my goggles and could see the sun just beginning to start a new day.

Tap ... tap ... tap.

Moving over to the window, I opened it to see Mikey standing on our front lawn. He was dressed like a mini GI Joe, in full fatigues, holding a long tree branch in both hands, ready to tap the window again.

"E-Ethan, E-Ethan, you'll never g-guess what I just saw," Mikey yelled up to me, jumping up and down.

"Slow down, Mikey. What is it?"

"T-Tony S. with another b-bike, and he headed over to Mr. G-Goodsmith's house. I saw them t-talking to each other, and then he l-left. I b-bet they're in this together, huh, E-Ethan? H-huh, ya think?"

Mikey was his old self again, I realized, as I watched him hopping around like a grasshopper. All memories of his recent self were quickly fading away.

"Wow, that's strange, and something that needs further sleuthing, Mikey, but we can't jump to any conclusions. We can't call it stealing till we have proof. That's supersleuthing 101," I said, trying to get Mikey to calm down.

"Get d-dressed in a h-hurry, and I'll go get A-Addison." Mikey turned around, running in the direction of her house, as I walked over to my closet to change.

Within minutes, I was dressed, washed up, and ready to go, and the tapping started again.

"I'll be right down," I yelled out the open window in my room. Addison and Mikey were standing below, Mikey still in jumping-jack mode. "And stop throwing those stones at my window. You break the glass, and Allymom won't be happy with any of us."

Heading downstairs, I heard Allymom typing away in the den. "Heading out, Allymom!" I shouted. "We're on a mission."

"We? Who's 'we,' Ethan?"

"Addison and Mikey and, of course, me—now known as the Supersleuth Gang," I yelled as I made my way into the kitchen, grabbing a bagel before I headed out the back door.

As the screen door slammed shut behind me, Allymom called out, "Well, tell the Supersleuth Gang I need to know what you're up to. I'm leaving by noon."

"Okay," I yelled back, hoping my response reached her as I started to run to meet up with my new gang.

"Hey, guys," I said. "We need to make a plan today—what we're going to do and all."

"Great idea," Addie said.

"Y-yeah," Mikey chimed in. "Let's go to my t-tree house. We can make that our new h-headquarters."

"Super idea. The tree house is the perfect cover zone for us, and no one will suspect anything. We need to be on the down low," I said as we all headed over to Mikey's house. I knew we needed a plan to get things in order and sort out all our intel so we would know what we needed to do and in what direction we were headed.

"You're so right," Addison said, blushing slightly, the color of her face almost matching her pink outfit.

Watching Addison, I thought, *Thank you, goggles, for allowing me to see this creature ... yeah!*

"Ethan, are you listening to me?"

"Yeah, yeah, yeah," I responded with a big smile on my face.

Climbing up the ladder to the tree house again brought back memories of Mikey and me, from when we were friends before.

"J-just like old t-times, huh, Ethan?" Mikey said, interrupting my same thoughts.

"Yeah, Mikey, just like old times, buddy." We both smiled, realizing things were back to how they used to be between us.

"It's good to see you two friends again," Addie said. "Really good."

"Okay, okay, let's get down to business," I said as I opened the folder I had brought along. It contained all the info we had on what had gone on so far. "There's a lot of work to be done here, and as Mrs. Pickens would say, there's no time to dawdle, lads."

We all laughed as we sat cross-legged in a circle on the tree-house floor and got down to business. I took out the printed pictures from the night before and laid them out on the floor in no particular order.

"Ethan, you know, if you move this picture into this position and this one here, and that one there ..." Addie rearranged my pictures like she was working on a jigsaw puzzle or playing a game of Scrabble.

"Wow, will you look at that?" I said. I could see a full bike coming into view as one picture was moved from one place to another.

"E-Ethan, E-Ethan, that looks like Johnny M-Miller's old bike," Mikey added.

"You know, I think you're right, but he's been riding a new bike lately. You know, he did say that one day his bike was stolen, and the next day, a brand-new bike was there. Guess that confirms everything that Detective Pardee told me. Johnny said he couldn't be happier, as his dad had been out of work and all for so long and had not been able to afford to buy him a new one for his birthday like he wanted. Johnny said there was a card attached to the bike, but only with the initials GSG. I wonder how this one landed in Mr. Goodsmith's hands."

"It's like right out of Robin Hood, huh, Ethan? I guess that's what we have to figure out—what part Mr. Goodsmith and Tony S. play in all this," Addison said. "What about these ones? Do these look familiar to anyone?"

"Hey, t-that looks l-like the b-bike that kid in Mrs. R-Reed's class used to r-r-ride. W-What's his n-name? K-Kirk something or other. But I haven't s-seen him with a b-bike lately, h-have y-you?"

"That's 'cause he has a cast on his ankle, Mikey. Duh!" Addison said. Her lack of patience with Mikey was sometimes so obvious.

"Oh, y-yeah, you're right, Addison. Duh is m-me," Mikey said, not catching on to her slight annoyance with him.

"Okay, gang, now we have some things to figure out. First, why are these bikes winding up with Mr. Goodsmith, how is he getting them, and what is Tony S.'s involvement? I think we have a good start and a lot of work to do."

The morning flew by as we worked on this mystery, and before we realized it, Mikey's mom was calling him in for lunch, the clang of her outside dinner bell alerting Mikey that he had about five minutes to get in the house or he was in trouble. That bell was so loud that it could be heard all around the neighborhood, and everyone who lived on our street knew its meaning.

One by one, we headed down the tree-house ladder. "Okay, supersleuth team, we'll meet back here in one hour, and then we'll head out to Mr. Goodsmith's house and back to see what Tony S. is doing. I'm going to call Detective Pardee and see if they have any other leads in the case. Be back here at 1:00 p.m. You snooze, you lose," I said with a laugh.

"R-roger th-that," Mikey said, heading into his house.

As Addison and I walked down the street to our houses, Tony S. zoomed by on his bike, waving to both of us.

"I don't know what's going on, but we're going to solve this puzzle. I just know it," I said.

"You will, Ethan. I mean, we all will. See you in a bit," Addison said as she left me at the end of my driveway and headed to her house.

"We will!" I yelled back to her, trying to convince myself of our success. Sergeant Bailey always told me success was the outcome of determination and knowledge, and as I entered the code to get in the back door of the house, I knew that at least we had the determination to solve this mystery, and I knew we were following a path that would help us get the rest.

CHAPTER 23

A GROWING SUSPECT LIST

After lunch I sat on our front porch steps, waiting for Addison and Mikey. The concrete felt cold on my hands even though it was warm outside—well, warm for the Buffalo area, at least. "Sixty-five degrees and sunny," the weatherman had said earlier.

Tony S. was coming up the street on his bike, this time with a small trailer attached to the back. There were two small bikes inside.

"Hey, Tony," I yelled from where I was sitting on the porch before he could say hello. "I'd know the sound of your bike a mile away."

Tony was pedaling fast, like he had somewhere urgent to go. "Yo, Ethan. You still wearing those crazy-looking goggles?" Tony S. asked. I watched him steer his bike up the driveway.

"Yeah, they make me look super cool, don't they? What's up?" I tried to sound easygoing so as not to raise any suspicions. I didn't want to slip up and say something that would divulge my new sightedness.

"Oh, just working on some old bikes, you know, but it's all for a good cause, for the kids and all."

"Oh, it is?" I said, trying to remain calm and cool.

"Yeah, yeah, Ethan. Why? You sound kind of like you're doubting me."

"Nah, Tony. Just heard that you've been seen with quite a few different bikes lately, and with all the commotion about missing bikes and all, I just didn't want to see you being a part of all that."

"Ethan, what are you accusing me of?" The look on Tony's face was hard to figure out. I couldn't tell if it was actual surprise or if he was trying to hide something.

"No, no, but you know, it does look suspicious and all, Tony S., especially with the police on alert and that article in the newspaper. Allymom says it's turning into something big. The people of this town want answers, and you know, that puts pressure on everyone."

"Trust me, Ethan—it's all good. If you want to come by and see, you know where I am. Well, I have to be on my way. Later."

Tony turned the bike and trailer around, and I had an unsettled feeling deep in my gut. I didn't know what to believe.

Just as he turned the corner, I saw Addison and Mikey coming from the other direction.

"You guys are never going to believe what just went down," I said when they reached the porch. I told them about my conversation with Tony S. "I think we have to go follow him now, since he seems to have an inventory building up. I swear, I don't know what to believe, but we can't go on suspicions. We need cold, hard facts if we're going to do this right."

"I agree, Ethan," Addison said.

Mikey shook his head in agreement. "E-Ethan, Jeff D-Dunkel just told me his b-bike went missing last n-night—you know, the b-blue racer, with that old-style b-banana-type seat—and just the o-other d-day, Laura's got taken from the school p-parking lot. She forgot to lock it up."

"No way," I said as we all started walking in the direction Tony S. was heading, more determined than ever to get to Tony S.'s area. "Voice-activate note taking."

"Note taking activated," said the voice. "Please advise when note taking is accomplished."

I repeated everything out loud that Tony S. and Mikey had told me and then advised the goggles, "Note taking completed."

"That is just too cool, Ethan," said Addison. "Gosh, I hate to agree with you on this one, Ethan, but I'm afraid you just may be right. Oh gosh, not Tony S." The look on her face spoke volumes.

"Well then, let's go and rule Tony S and Pete out as our top suspects," I said.

"Yes, Ethan," the voice responded. "Suspect list created, and Pete added. There are now three suspects on this list: Mr. Goodsmith, Tony S., and Pete. File saved and closed."

As we made our way down the street, we looked like quite a team. In 3-D, everything looked that much clearer and more detailed—Mikey in his GI Joe uniform, Addie in royal blue, and me with my goggles. We were quite a sight to be seen.

CHAPTER 24

CLUES FROM TONY S.

The three of us walked arm in arm down the street until we arrived at the area where Tony S. lived. He never wanted to stay in a shelter; he said he felt too confined. I never could understand that, but then again, I hadn't experienced the things that Tony S. had in his life. The city had even offered him a small trailer for free once, but he had refused. I guess he lived his life in a way that worked for him.

All three of us got down on our hands and knees and peered over the embankment, down into the area Tony S. called home. Again, we saw quite a collection of bikes and tools. Tony S. was working hard at disassembling the bike in front of him, with Rusty, his dog, at his side. Rusty had lived on the streets too, alone, before he met Tony S. They had now been together for years, as close to each other as I was to Tucker.

"Look, E-Ethan. Isn't that J-Jeff's racer, the blue one, with the white-striped b-banana seat leaning against the w-wall? And look, there's P-Pete steering what looks just like L-Laura's bike down the h-hill."

We watched as Pete reached the landing and started talking to Tony S.

"I can't hear what they're saying. Can either of you?" Addison asked.

"Voice, can we get clearer audio?" I said.

Addie and Mikey looked at me like I was crazy for asking the goggles.

"Hey, you never know what these things can do until you ask," I said.

"Audio enhanced," the voice responded. Immediately, we were able to hear the conversation below through the goggles.

"Tony, look at this bike," Pete said. "Ain't it a beauty?"

"It'll be perfect for the project," Tony said.

"Saw Mr. Goodsmith on my way here. He said it was just lying on the grass, ready for trash pickup tomorrow. No one was around, no kids or nothin', so he took it; it will be a great addition to our project."

"Seems strange and all that it would just be lying there, Pete. Is this on the up-and-up? Are you not telling me something?"

"Hey, man, back off. What are you accusing me of? I ain't no stealer or robber. I'm telling ya the truth."

Rusty started to growl at Pete, forever the protector of Tony S. It was like there was some rule of the streets that Rusty knew too.

"I'm not accusing you of nothing yet, Pete. We're meeting with Goodsmith tonight at seven, and I'm gonna get some answers."

"This does not look good, guys," I said, looking down at the ground, my head hanging low. "Whatever they're up to, it's up to us to figure it out, right?"

"Oh, Ethan." Addison put her hand on my shoulder. "I'm afraid you might be right. What should we do now, go call the police?"

"No, we have to find out the connection between these bikes and Mr. Goodsmith. Let's meet up again at six forty-five and head back over to Mr. Goodsmith's house. I'm not sure this solves anything for us yet."

"G-good, because I'm s-starving," Mikey said. "I need to get back before my mom starts clanging that bell and embarrassing me in front of the whole neighborhood."

"Oh, Mikey, you'd better run, then," Addie said with a laugh. "See you all later."

As we all headed in the direction of our own houses, I passed Mr. Goodsmith's and saw him standing in the picture window, staring me down. Then I realized I was still wearing the goggles, but for some reason, it felt like something more. His eyes were fixated on me like some sort of scanner, like he was looking right through me; actually, it felt like he was looking right inside my head, into my brain, and he could read my every thought. I caught myself with my hand in midair to wave at him just as he turned away. He was gone from my view, only the fluttering of the curtain signaling his departure. The moment left me feeling out of sorts and confused. Things seemed to be adding up, just like one of Mr. Bleyle's math equations. But for some reason, I didn't feel like this equation was adding up the way I wanted it to.

"What is going on?" I said out loud.

The voice answered, "Solve the mystery, and you will have your answer, Ethan."

I nodded my head and stayed silent. I headed in the only direction I knew to turn at this time: home.

CHAPTER 25

SUPERSLEUTH GANG

As usual, I was lost in my thoughts as I walked inside the house, still wearing the goggles.

"I'm beginning to get used to this new look, Ethan," Allymom said with a smile on her face.

I swallowed quickly, looking down at my feet as I made my way into the kitchen, hoping she wouldn't read the shock on my face and somehow realize that I could see her.

"I ... I just found these the other day, I told you," I responded, hoping to make it sound like they were just another toy. "Or at least I thought I did."

"Yes, you did, but it is still a sight to be seen, my sweet." Allymom was always the reporter on duty, even when she was just Allymom. She loved solving things almost as much as I did. I guess we were a lot alike in that way. Moms are like that, anyway—detectives, always solving their own little mysteries when it has to do with their kids. Nothing got past Allymom without some degree of suspicion, so I knew I had to play this the right way.

"You know us kids, always looking for something new and fun. If it's not a new video game, new paraphernalia always fits the bill." I plastered a big grin on my face, one of those smiles where just about every tooth in your mouth is showing. From the look on Allymom's face, I wasn't sure she was buying into my story.

"*Paraphernalia.* My oh my, now that's a very interesting word."

"Yep, see how I'm getting a good edu-ma-cation? So what's for dinner?" I said, hoping to change the subject. "Something sure smells good."

"Nothing's for dinner till you wash those grimy hands. Just where have you been all day, Ethan?"

"Oh, you know, just having fun with my gang," I said.

"The gang, is it?" Allymom laughed.

"Oh yeah, Mikey and I patched things up. Isn't that great? So we're calling ourselves the Supersleuth Gang—Mikey, Addison, and yours truly." I laughed a big, hearty laugh, hoping it would help. "And since I have these goggles, I've been deemed the Goggles Master."

"Okay. Well, Goggles Master, please go wash your nasty hands before you eat dinner. Wings and potato skins are in your near future."

I headed toward the stairs quickly, hoping to avoid any more questions. I let out a big sigh of relief when no more came. Silence, golden silence.

I walked into my bedroom, my safe haven, and took a big leap and flopped on my bed for just a moment, letting thoughts of the days play out in my head. For some reason, I thought better with the goggles on. Strange.

"Ethan, you eating tonight or not?"

I realized I was taking too long. "Coming, Allymom."

Dinner went by without a hitch, and the subject of the goggles didn't come up while we were eating, even though I wore them while we ate. I figured the more I wore them, the less out of place they would be and the less frequent the questions would be. *Phew!* I thought. It was hard to keep a straight face with all this excitement, let alone while staring right at Allymom and seeing her in 3-D. It almost felt like a dream, a really good dream.

"Ethan, you know, I can see my reflection clear as day in those goggles," Allymom said.

Gulping loudly, I thought, *I can see you clear as day too!* I knew I had to change the subject and change it quickly. My eyes blinked rapidly as I tried to think of something to say. "These are the best wings, Allymom. Buffalo, the home of the wings—I guess that's our claim to fame here, right?"

"Yes, our claim to fame, Ethan. Now finish up."

"By the way, the gang's picking me up at six forty-five, and we're all going to hang out tonight for a while, it being vacation and all. That okay with you, Allymom?"

"Sure. You know your curfew time, Ethan, and you know the ramifications of not being here when you should."

"I know, I know. It's, like, written in stone somewhere, right?" I said, smiling. Wearing the goggles made it so much easier to understand Allymom because her reactions all played out on her face. She was smiling, and smiling from my mom was always a good thing in my book, whether I saw it on her face or heard it in her words. Either way, it was all good.

"Yes, it's a big stone tablet locked up in a vault in the basement, the sacred plaque of mom rules. It's centuries old," Allymom said, playing along with me.

"Well, one of these days, you'll have to show me that sacred plaque so I can confirm these rules are real."

"Oh, don't you worry yourself, Ethan. Those rules are real, plaque or no plaque." We both laughed as we stood up at the same time to clear our plates.

"You wash; I'll dry. Hmm, plaque rule number 144. That sure must be a big plaque, because gosh knows there sure are plenty of house rules."

"And best you not forget, my dear Goggles Master," Allymom said, just as the back doorbell rang. "Your Supersleuth Gang awaits. Go on now. I'll finish up here, Ethan."

"Thanks," I said as I opened the door and walked out, looking back just to see her smiling again. Ah, life was finally coming together for me. Life was good.

CHAPTER 26

TONAWANDA PD

Addison and Mikey were waiting for me when I got outside. Time seemed to be moving faster than a locomotive, and we needed to stay on top of things. We all quickened our pace as we headed over to Mr. Goodsmith's house, hoping to get there before Tony S. and Pete. Time was crucial, as our curfews played a big part in our mission. As we walked along, I began to play the question over and over again in my mind: "What was this all about?"

Just as we got into our hiding place in the bushes just to the left of Mr. Goodsmith's front door, we saw Tony S. and Pete, each riding a bicycle and heading up the driveway. Mr. Goodsmith came out onto his porch just as Tony S. and Pete made their way up the porch steps. The men shook hands, and the conversation between them was short. They talked about new inventory and how great sales were. Mr. Goodsmith pointed out to the men the new wind chimes he had put up on his porch and that sales of these specific wind chimes were soaring.

Just then, the voice interrupted what was going on. "Incoming thought message," it whispered into my left ear.

"Incoming what?" I said softly but out loud.

"W-Who you t-talking to, E-Ethan?" Mikey asked.

Before I could answer, another voice was heard coming from the goggles, whispering to me into my left ear, "Listen and learn, Ethan; put all the pieces together, and you will have enough to solve this puzzle."

The second voice I heard sounded just like Mr. Goodsmith, and as I looked back to the porch, I could see him again, looking right in the direction of where we were hiding. How did he know?

"Ethan, you okay?" Addison said. "You look like you've just seen a ghost."

I stayed silent and nodded my head, signaling I was okay. The goggles recorded everything and took pictures to back it all up. Tony S. and Pete got back on their bikes and headed off in the direction they had come from.

"What does this all mean?" I whispered to Addison and Mikey. They both shrugged their shoulders in unison.

"I think I need to notify Detective Pardee when I get back home; hopefully, I'll catch him tonight. He works the second shift every now and then; well, at least that's what Allymom told me before when she worked with him on a story for the newspaper."

"Well, let us know what he says, Ethan. I guess we should head home," Addison responded.

As we walked the short distance back to my house, we were all silent until we said our good-byes and Addison and Mikey headed off in the direction of their houses. The streetlights signaled our curfew time had approached.

I knew that Detective Pardee would want evidence, and it was piling up, so the first thing I did when I got inside was head right to the phone and dial the number for the police department, hoping to catch him.

"Hello. Tonawanda PD. Is this an emergency?"

"Uh ... well, yes and no. I need to speak to Detective Pardee, if I could. This is Ethan Pero. We're sort of working a case together," I said to the dispatch lady.

"Oh, Ethan, I didn't recognize you. This is Miss Cantino. I'll see if he's in; let me place you on hold." Miss Cantino lived around the block from us. She and Allymom had gone to high school together. I didn't know her all that well, but for some reason, everyone seemed to know me.

While I waited for Detective Pardee to pick up the phone, I reviewed all the evidence. We had a pretty good file, and all fingers pointed at three likely suspects.

"Ethan, dear, Detective Pardee is in a meeting. Would you like his voice mail so you can leave him a message?" Ms. Cantino said.

"Sure, I guess."

"Okay, hold on, and I'll connect you to his voice mail."

"Hello, this is Detective Pardee. I'm away from my desk. Please leave me a message, and I'll contact you back." The usual beeps played until it was my turn to leave a message.

"Detective Pardee, this is Ethan Pero. We talked before about the missing bikes in the area. Well, I have quite a file collected, and I have some suspicions that are leading to three possible suspects."

I went on to tell him about my suspect list, which included Mr. Goodsmith. Mr. Goodsmith was such an icon in the town and a good man, and I knew that the town would have a hard time believing he could be involved in all this, but I was sure he must have his reasons.

"Please call me as soon as you can. Some things just don't add up, but it doesn't look at all good. If you would like to see all my evidence—" The line cut me off before I could finish. I guess I had talked long enough.

I hung up the phone and walked over to the fridge to get a can of soda. *All this sleuthing sure makes me thirsty,* I thought. My throat felt as dry as the Sahara Desert. The phone rang just as I took the last gulp from the can, and I moved quickly to answer it on the second ring.

"Hello," I said into the phone.

"Ethan, this is Detective Pardee. I heard your message. Sounds like you're turning into James Bond right before my eyes. That's quite a mission you've been on. Why don't you come down to the station and show me all that evidence you've talked about?"

"Now? Right now?" I asked with nervous anticipation.

"Now seems as good a time as ever, Ethan. See you in a few." And he hung up.

Since we were all to meet at Addie's house later, I called her and let her know I was going to be late and why. Immediately after hanging up the phone, I headed out toward the police station.

"Boy, someone's in a hurry to get somewhere quick." Mr. Smergle was sitting in his usual spot on his porch, Lucy spread lazily at his feet.

"If you only knew, Mr. Smergle. If you only knew," I said as I quickened my pace, hoping to avoid any questions. Luckily, no one else in the neighborhood was out.

I arrived at the police station in record time. The automatic doors opened as I approached the door, and as I saw my reflection in the glass, I realized I had not taken the goggles off before I left. A man was standing just inside the doorway.

"Quite a pair of goggles, Mr. Bond," Detective Pardee said with a chuckle.

"They do seem to be the talk of the town lately, Detective," I said, hoping to avoid any further suspicion regarding the goggles.

"So let's go to my office and see all your evidence."

Detective Pardee guided me by the arm through the twists and turns of the police station hallways. When we stopped in front of his office and he opened the door, thankfully, the voice stayed quiet.

"Here, Ethan, have a seat," he said as he led me to the chair.

I sat down and said, "Now, my team has gathered most of this intel, and we've discussed it all, and it looks highly suspicious."

"That's quite a file you have there, Ethan. I'd like to bring my sergeant in to see all this."

The detective walked into the next room and then came back with another man walking behind him.

"Sarge, this is Ethan Pero—you know, Allison's son. Well, he has compiled quite the case on the missing bikes, and I want you to look it all over."

As Detective Pardee went through the case file with the sergeant, I could see that they were both impressed by the work we had done.

"Okay, Ethan, let us look at all this in more detail," said the detective, "and we'll be in touch. Can I see you out? You need some help?"

"Thanks, Detective. I can see my way out," I said, smiling. I walked out of his office and back outside, thinking, *If you only knew.*

CHAPTER 27

FIGURING THINGS OUT

As soon as I exited, I almost ran into Mikey, who was waiting for me outside the police station. "Hey, Mikey," I said.

This time, Mikey was wearing a different outfit. I suspected that he was trying to be Neo from *The Matrix*, or what I thought Neo would have looked like. He was dressed in all black, with black glasses and a cape.

"Great outfit," I said as Mikey whirled about in a circle, his cape flowing around him.

"I'm th-thinking, I l-like this one a bit b-better than the other one. What do ya th-think, E-Ethan?"

"Yep, that's definitely your new look."

Mikey spread his arms again, wide open, and this time, the wind caught his cape, and he looked like he would soar up to the sky at any moment. "My mom just sh-shook her h-head when she s-saw me. You'd think by now she would be used to my d-dramatics, right? I g-got a y-yellow cape for you t-too, Ethan. Here, t-try it on."

I grabbed the cape from Mikey, tied the string around my neck to hold it in place, and spun around in a circle.

"What's all that laughing about? I'm beginning to feel left out," Addison said, walking toward us.

"Oh, nothing, Addison, or at least nothing to worry yourself over. Just the caped crusaders having a good laugh about our new costumes."

"Neo, in living color—well, in black and white, at least—and none other than the Goggles Master," Addison responded, and we all started to laugh.

This felt like old times again, when the three of us were all good buddies. Mrs. Pickens talked about "old times." She said they were the times, as friends, that people would always remember, even when they were like her, old and gray. "Memories last a lifetime, Ethan," she had said. Before, I didn't really know what she was talking about, but now things were different, and I was realizing these were going to be the memories I long remembered.

But it was time to get back to business. This was the here and now, with no time to waste, and things needed to get done and solved. Leaving the police building, we all moved quickly down the sidewalk toward our final destination. The medley of greetings began as we moved through our neighborhood, as was usual in our small town.

The voice identified all the neighbors to me, and I was grateful to finally have faces to put with all these voices after all these years.

"Nice goggles, Ethan," yelled Mr. Smergle from across the street. His cat, Lucy, was sitting on his front porch swing. I got a better look at her this time. She was a beauty, her long tail swaying along with the slow movement of the porch swing. She was a Maine Coon, Mr. Smergle had told me long ago.

"My, my, aren't you all quite the sight?" Mrs. Frangle yelled to us as she continued to water her lawn with the hose. All her flower beds were in full bloom. The colors of the flowers matched the scents I had known all these years. It was a rainbow of colors, all right.

"*Buon giorno* to all of you," Mrs. Catalano said in her soft voice. She was picking tomatoes, no doubt for that night's pasta sauce. The smells of basil and oregano filled the air.

Mr. Goodsmith's property was just a few houses down. It was still light out, and that could be a definite problem for our mission.

"Hey, why don't we hang out at the playground for a few, until the sun goes down and the streetlights go on? That will give us less of a chance of being seen," I said to the gang.

"Sure, Ethan," Addison and Mikey responded in unison, and we turned around and made the short trek to the playground.

By the sounds of voices, I could tell lots of kids were at the playground, even from a distance. We arrived in no time, and Addie played her role and guided me to where all our friends were. We still had to put on a show for them even though I could see all of them clearly.

"Hey, guys!" I yelled out.

"Ethan, watch yourself. Remember, to all of them you're still blind," Addison said, nudging me in the ribs.

"Ouch, that hurt." I looked straight at her and laughed. "Be nice."

"Now, Laura and Jeff are straight ahead, and Brian and Shira are on their left."

"Hey!" the kids all responded at varying times.

"Laura and Jeff, is it true your bikes were taken the other day?" I asked.

"Yeppers," Jeff answered.

Laura nodded in agreement and said, "But the strangest thing was new bikes showed up at each of our houses the next day, and boy, our parents were thrilled, especially our dads. You know, they're both still out of work, with the closing of the plant."

"That is s-super s-strange," Mikey said. "S-super-d-duper strange."

"Well, about as strange as those goggles Ethan has on," Brian said. "What's up with those, Ethan?"

"Oh, these old things. Just something I found the other day. Neat, aren't they?" I said.

"*Neat* is not the word. Those are awesome," Brian said.

"Yeah, I think they're one of a kind, just like me," I said with a grin.

The groans from my biggest fans could be heard all around, and we all laughed.

I sat on one of the benches that encircled the playground, watching everyone play for a while. The goggles detailed it all for me: Addison on the swing, her legs propelling her back and forth; Mikey coming down headfirst on the slide, stopping just short of falling to the ground; and Brian showing all his "muscles" on the monkey bars, as he moved across them easily, with little to no effort. I was learning quickly about all the things that were everyday occurrences in my life, and I think that's what made it less difficult for me that I wasn't able to join in and play too. *One day*, I thought, *I might be able to do all those things too.*

"Well, it's getting dark, gang. Guess we all should be heading home," Addie said with a wink and a glance in Mikey's and my direction.

"Yep," Mikey said.

"Later, guys," I said as we turned and made our way out of the playground. We headed back in the direction of Mr. Goodsmith's house. None of the neighbors was out this time, which made our getting there that much easier. "It's a good thing we all wore dark colors today. Hopefully, we'll blend right into the shadows—less chance of being discovered by anyone," I said as we bent down low in the bushes.

Just as we settled into our hiding place, Tony S. flew by on his bike. We watched him pedal up Mr. Goodsmith's driveway.

"Guess we're right on time," Addison said, looking at her watch.

"Timing is everything," I said.

We watched from the shadows of the bushes in front of Mr. Goodsmith's house. Tony S. stepped up onto the porch and was soon joined by Mr. Goodsmith.

"Audio enhancement, please," I commanded the goggles.

"So it looks like everything is going as planned," Tony S. said to Mr. Goodsmith.

"So it is, Tony. So it is." Mr. Goodsmith appeared to be looking over Tony S.'s shoulder when he talked, exactly in our direction.

"Well, I couldn't be happier with my part in this, and to be honest, I like the work, and I like the money, and I like keeping busy. Thanks for helping me out with all this, Mr. Goodsmith." Tony S. sounded prouder than I had ever heard him. "All those bikes are landing in the hands of those less fortunate."

"Good work, Tony. Glad I could help out. See you soon, all right?"

We watched as they shook hands. Tony S. walked off the porch, and Mr. Goodsmith went back into the house.

This was my chance to get some answers. Before Tony S. could get back on his bike, I leaped out from our hiding place with a big "Aha!"

"Aha yourself, Ethan," Tony S. responded.

"Caught right in the scheme of things, huh, Tony?"

"Whatcha talkin' about, Ethan?"

"You know exactly what I'm talking about, Tony—the bike-stealing scheme. How could you?"

"It ain't what it looks like, Ethan, and you're traveling down an uncharted road with these accusations, young man," Tony said sternly, like a father.

"So, Tony, then you tell me what's going on. Give me the lowdown, then. Tell me the scoop. Fill in the blanks," I said in my toughest voice.

"Okay, here goes. You know my situation, right? Well, I get a monthly stipend from my years in the service and all. That's how I try to survive, but it ain't much. So Mr. Goodsmith was kind enough to give me some used bikes, those that people discarded. I take 'em apart, or I just fix them up, all shiny and new. The shiny and new ones, I sell those to Old Man Sills. You know, he has that bike shop over there on Bailey Avenue, down the street from that beef-on-weck place and across the street from the Garden of Sweets. He pays me, and he sells the bikes at a discounted price to people who can't pay the full amount. So it works for both of us. So ya see, Ethan, even with those snazzy goggles you got there, things aren't always what they seem to be. Let that be a life lesson learned. Ah, you young'uns, you got a lot to learn in this life."

With that, Tony S. got on his bike and headed down the street. With a honk and a wave, he was gone, leaving me standing there, realizing our suspect list had just got smaller, and we were no closer to solving our mystery.

CHAPTER 28

MISSION ACCOMPLISHED

"Guess we were barking up the wrong tree, as Mrs. Pickens would say, huh, gang?"

Addison and Mikey stood up from their spot in the bushes. Addison nodded in agreement, and Mikey just stood there, looking sad and dejected.

"I just hope we didn't lose Tony S. as a friend, accusing him of stealing and all," I said. "That would be terrible."

"That would be awful, Ethan," Addison responded, "but I have a feeling he'll be okay. It's just a hunch, but my hunches are usually right, and in his life, I'm sure he's used to the ups and downs of it all."

"So our suspect list has got a bit smaller because I guess we can cross Tony S. off the list and Pete as well. Am I right?"

"L-looks that w-way, E-Ethan," Mikey said.

"I guess so," Addison added.

Just then, we heard a screen door slam shut, and we turned to see Mr. Goodsmith heading down the concrete steps of his porch in the direction of his parked car. In each of his hands, he was holding onto a suitcase.

"Where are you going, Mr. Goodsmith?" I yelled to him from where we were standing at the end of his long driveway.

"You know how it is, or maybe you don't, Ethan. Places to go, people to see, young man."

"How long are you going to be gone? When are you coming back?" I questioned.

"Now that there is a good question, Ethan. I guess time will tell," Mr. Goodsmith responded, staring off into the distance. "Gonna travel the world, but you'll be hearing from me real soon. Don't you worry none."

Before I could answer him, Mr. Goodsmith got into his car, pulled out of the driveway, and headed down the street. Hanging in the back window of his car, swaying in the breeze created by the open window, were the bike wind chimes. A sign on his back bumper lit up at the same time his brake lights came on: "Mission Accomplished."

I looked over at Addison and Mikey, whose faces seemed to reflect the same look of surprise that was surely on my face too.

"Mission complete," the voice confirmed. The voice then proceeded to tell us all about Mr. Goodsmith's role in all this as we watched his car disappear around the corner.

We got our man, I thought as the voice explained.

All three of us stood there, glued to our spots, mouths hanging open, as Mr. Goodsmith seemingly drove out of our lives.

"Let's go home," I said.

Addie and Mikey shook their heads, and we all made the trek home in silence.

CHAPTER 29

THE END OF A MYSTERY

"Ethan, I need to talk to you," Allymom yelled up to me.

"Be right down," I said, thinking back over the last few days and wondering what trouble I had got myself into to make her need to talk to me. I grabbed my goggles from their hiding place and headed out of my room.

Allymom was standing at the bottom of the stairs as I made my way down, taking each step one at a time. "Ethan, Detective Pardee called me. We had quite the conversation about you and all that you've been up to lately. He gave me quite a detailed account about the bikes, the chimes, Mr. Goodsmith, Tony S., and Pete's involvement in this whole mystery. That sure is a lot of detective work you got done, my little supersleuth—well, with the help of your little posse."

"Wow, he said all that. That rocks. I guess I'm the town's little hero, you could say," I said with a big smirk on my face, letting her know I was just teasing her with my comment.

"Okay, my little hero, make sure you can get that head through your bedroom door." And we both laughed as she teased me right back.

Allymom told me that the police had got a task force together, which had headed over to Mr. Goodsmith's house, where they had found more evidence that led to a full investigation, but Mr. Goodsmith, of course, was nowhere to be found. There were more than twenty envelopes in a neat pile on the kitchen table, addressed to each of the individuals whose bikes had been taken recently, with a gift certificate inside for the purchase of a new bike. Otherwise, things were strewn all over his house, with drawers and closets open, dishes in the sink, and the bed unmade. But there was no sign of him.

Just then the doorbell rang, and Allymom went to the front door. There was Detective Pardee standing on the porch. Allymom let him into the living room.

"Well, Son, you solved the case." I realized that Detective Pardee was here to congratulate me. He took my hand in his, shook it, and said that there would be a ceremony the next day honoring me, and with that, he left just as quickly as he had come in.

"Quite the journey you've been on, Ethan, one you should be quite proud of," said Allymom, "now I know what all those nighttime outings have been about."

"I do want to apologize if I haven't been totally up front with you, Allymom, but as you can see, it was all in the best interest of the whole town," I said, hoping she wasn't going to be too mad at me.

"I guess I should be upset that you haven't been exactly honest with me, but in the end, I see it worked out all right. In the future, I hope you know you can confide in me," Allymom said with a little sadness in her voice.

I hoped I hadn't hurt her feelings.

But then she added, "I guess you're gonna be a little supersleuth and follow in your Allymom's footsteps." She chuckled a bit and headed back into the kitchen, stopping at the credenza by the kitchen door. "Oh, by the way, this came addressed to you in the mail today. Were you expecting something? It feels like a disc of some sort. If you need help with it, let me know. I'm going to start on dinner," she said as she grabbed my left hand and placed the envelope in my palm, my fingers closing around it and holding it tight.

"Okay, will do," I said, eager to find out just what could be inside this package. I made my way back upstairs to my room, this time taking two steps at a time. I was only eleven, so getting mail was not something that happened to me a lot. I got out my goggles and opened the envelope. It was a CD disc. *Strange*, I thought. *Who would be sending me a disc?*

There was no letter or anything else inside the envelope, and there was no label on the disc. I went to my laptop and inserted it into the slot. After a moment, I heard Mr. Goodsmith's voice, loud and deep.

> *Good job, young man. I see you found those goggles to be an asset. They were helpful when Mrs. Pickens and I were your age and found them in her parents' house, the same house she lives in now. We had quite the missions in our day too. Know that this was your first mission, but not your last. There will be more mysteries to solve. I will be away for a while, but I will be in touch. Good-bye for now, Ethan. Congrats to you and your team.*

That was it—a few short words and then dead silence.

CHAPTER 30

MY SHINY NEW FUTURE

My future was now a story waiting to be written, and I felt good knowing the goggles would be a part of all of it, but even more, I felt good that Mr. Goodsmith was still my friend.

The following evening, Allymom took me and my gang to the ceremonial presentation at city hall. She made me wear my suit and tie, which felt constricting and stiff.

When it was time for the ceremony to begin, I heard Mayor McGurren's voice from the stage. "Good Evening to everyone who has come to celebrate in the honoring of Ethan, Addison, and Mikey for solving our latest dilemma here in Tonawanda. We are here to present hero's badges to all three of these outstanding citizens for solving the missing-bicycles mystery. Come on up, you three."

Addison grabbed my hand and led me to the stage. I could feel the sweat beginning to build.

"Stay cool, Ethan. It's just little old me."

"That does seem to be a problem when I'm around you," I teased back, and I felt the familiar nudge in my ribs before I finished my sentence.

"Oh, sh-shush, you t-two. You both kn-know you have a c-crush on each other. Just a-admit it," Mikey said.

"Oh, shush, Mikey," we both said at once.

I was happy I wasn't wearing the goggles to the ceremony. I really didn't want to see Addison's reaction. But she gave my hand a little squeeze in response to Mikey's words, which felt like the reassurance I needed that she liked me just as much as I liked her, and for now, that was enough.

The mayor presented all three of us with our badges, pinning them to our chests, and told us that a plaque with our names on it, stating we were all honorary junior detectives, would be hung in city hall. He went on to tell us that the townspeople had lined up at city hall to defend Mr. Goodsmith as the town's very own Robin Hood. No one wanted to press charges, and without charges, nothing further was to be done. Case closed.

"Wow, what a great-looking plaque, Ethan. You should see it," Addie said. It sounded like she was beaming.

"Ethan, can you step forward?" the mayor requested.

I walked forward, with a little help from Addie.

"Ethan, we are also presenting you with a key to the city for being the central figure in getting this mystery solved for us. You are quite the supersleuth, I have to say."

"Thank you, sir, and thanks to everyone who came out to be with me and my friends!" I yelled out to the crowd, lifting the key over my head. It felt large and heavy in my arms, but at this moment, that didn't matter.

The cheers and applause were deafening, but I stood there smiling the whole time as I listened to the crowd chanting my name. Mixed in with the chants were compliments and expressions of disbelief.

"Ethan, Ethan, Ethan!"

"Can you believe Ethan solved the case?"

"I can't believe our Ethan did this."

"He's a hero. I always knew he was special."

"Wow, this is so epic. Ethan Pero—who would have guessed?"

Allymom took all of us to Friendly's ice cream shop afterward, and we each had a banana split with extra whipped cream and cherries. I was the talk of the town, which was buzzing with all the excitement over how I had helped solve the case. By the time we got home, I was exhausted, and I headed to my room.

"Night, Allymom. This supersleuth needs a super-duper sleep."

I closed my bedroom door behind me, relishing in the peaceful sound of nothingness.

CONCLUSION

Lying on my bed in my room, I could feel the heat on my face from the light overhead. It felt warm and comforting, like a hot cup of cocoa with whipped-cream topping. I didn't have to see the light or drink the cocoa to get the feeling. I just had to think about it and feel the warmth. That's how good memories are. They create "memory feelings," those warm feelings that you get just thinking about something that happened in the past—something good, something worth remembering, just like Mrs. Pickens said.

I suspected that's how I would feel later when I thought back on this time. I had done it—well, the Supersleuth Gang had done it, but I had been a part of it. This felt good because it wasn't something that someone had told me to do or expected me to do. It hadn't felt like a chore or a homework assignment. I had done my part with the help of a great supersleuth team.

The light shining on my face made me feel like a star, like I was important—a hero! We had solved the case, and it was all good. I felt good. A superhero, cape-waving, standing-tall-with-chest-puffed-out type of good. I finally had done something to be really proud of, with a little help, of course, from the goggles and the voice. But that's our little secret for now. I started something, and we finished it. It was an open-and-shut case.

My hand sought out the badge on my chest that the police had given me. Addie had described it to me—all pointy, shiny, and gold. I wanted to create the visual memory all on my own. The memory would always stay with me. I would treasure it and tuck it away and bring it out from time to time.

So I was hooked. I wanted to do it again, and soon. I could do it again. I had the skills and the tools and the gang: Addison and Mikey. I had gained my best friend back. Life was good, Mrs. Pickens always said, through the good times and the bad. I now knew what she meant by that, and she was so right.

I decided I didn't want to wear the goggles all the time. Sometimes I liked my sightless world. It was quieter—less input, less static, less noise, if that makes any sense—without all the visual stimulation and chaos that was so new to me. And this minute, I wanted quiet. I wanted to soak in my newfound celebrity without any distractions. I wanted to relish my five minutes of fame all alone, in the quiet of my own world. Ethan Pero, a crime solver, an investigator extraordinaire, a case closer.

I thought about the book I had found at Mrs. Pickens's house and the cavernous hole. I never had found the time to look more into those things. Most of the pages of the book had gone unread, and I'd never found the time to search the area in Mrs. Pickens's house more, since the mystery of the missing bikes had kept me so busy. But those were things for another time, another day. My future was in front of me, and I had all the time in the world.

I reached for the book in my backpack and felt the softness of the cover. I held it close to my chest and knew this book had been meant for me, and only me, to find, and I just knew it held more exciting things for me to learn. I was a supersleuth now. I had the goggles, and I had the book. My Batcave was yet to be searched, but I knew everything was safe for now. It could wait. It would wait for me.

I began to wonder when Mr. Goodsmith would get in touch with me, but I knew he would. I knew that could wait too.

I reached underneath my pillow. The metal of the goggles was cool against my fingers, and it brought a smile to my face. I put the goggles on and opened the book to the first few pages, where I had left off. The voice helped me understand the areas I needed help in, as the words revealed the possibility of another mystery to me and my role in it, if I chose to accept the challenge. The sound from my computer signaling the arrival of a new e-mail interrupted my thoughts, and when I looked at the screen and saw the e-mail address including the name *Goodsmith*, well, in that single moment, it hit me: I was going to be all right. I could finally see my future, and it was all shiny and bright—3-D bright.

CPSIA information can be obtained at www.ICGtesting.com
Printed in the USA
LVOW08s0852141015

458105LV00002B/3/P